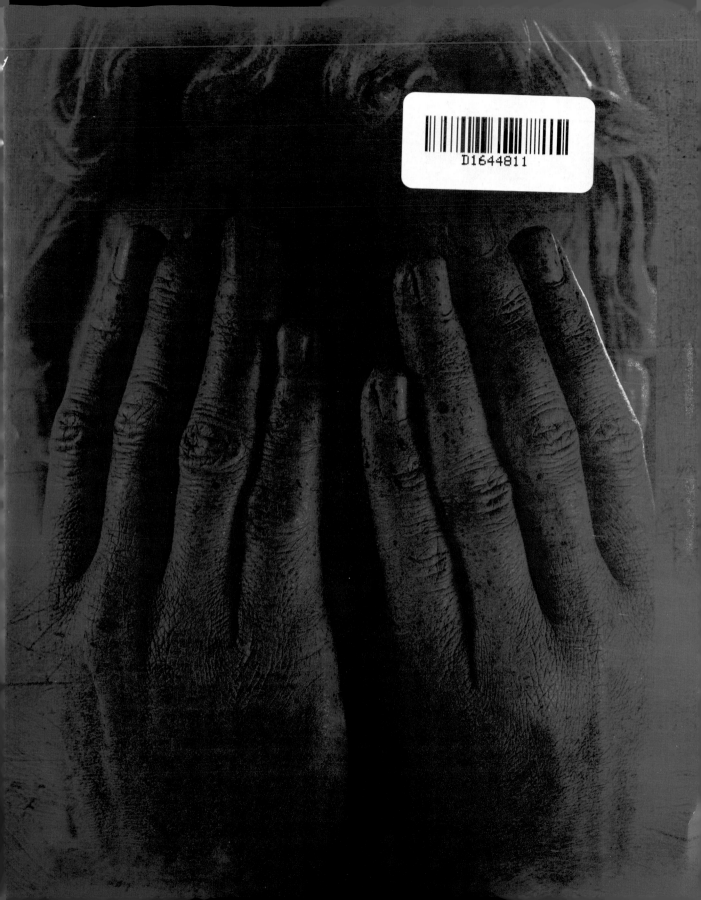

BBC CHILDREN'S BOOKS

UK | USA | Canada | Ireland | Australia

India | New Zealand | South Africa

BBC Children's Books are published by Puffin Books, part of the Penguin Random House group of companies whose addresses can be found at global.penguinrandomhouse.com.

puffinbooks.com

Penguin
Random House
UK

First published by Puffin Books 2013

001

Written by Justin Richards

Printed in China.

A CIP catalogue record for this book is available from the British Library.

BBC

DOCTOR WHO

100

SCARIEST MONSTERS

CONTENTS

All the Strange, Strange Creatures...

Over the years, across the universe, the Doctor has encountered all manner of alien creatures.
Some of them have been friendly, but many others have been **ruthless** monsters.
This book is about those monsters.
Despite the huge variety of these monsters, they all have two things in common –
they are seriously **frightening**,
and they have **all** been defeated by **the Doctor**.
This book brings together a hundred of the very **scariest monsters** the Doctor has faced.
It's not a contest – they aren't in order of scariness.
Just as the Doctor has found, the monsters appear when they choose,
perhaps when you **least expect them**.
And after all, who is to say that meeting a **Dalek** is more or less scary than encountering
a **Cyberman**, or a **Weeping Angel**, or one of the Adherents of the **Repeated Meme?**
It depends on the circumstances,
it depends if there's any **way of escape**,
and it depends what you are **frightened** of.
But whatever **scares** you – it's in here, hiding within these pages.
There's only **one** thing that's more certain.
And that's the fact that there are sure to be even more, even scarier monsters **still** out there,
waiting for the Doctor.

And

**waiting
for you.**

Weeping Angels

Nicknamed 'Weeping Angels' because of the form they so often take, the Lonely Assassins are an ancient race of killers, as old as the universe itself. They absorb time energy from their victims – sending them into the past, and taking the energy of the days they never lived.

The Weeping Angels are especially dangerous, as when you look at them, they are just stone statues. But this is a defence mechanism, and if you so much as blink, a Weeping Angel can move to attack.

The Tenth Doctor and Martha were sent back in time by the touch of an Angel, but helped by Sally Sparrow. At the wreck of the *Byzantium*, the Doctor and Amy, together with River Song, were attacked by an army of Weeping Angels.

Origin
Unknown

Doctors Encountered
Tenth, Eleventh

Description
Statues in the form of angels

Fear Factor
10/10

The Silence

Origin
Unknown

Doctors Encountered
Eleventh

Description
No one remembers what they look like

But what the Silence want, *why* they were here, remains a mystery. It is a mystery that the Doctor must solve – if he is to save the world. If he is to save his own life . . .

The Silence were among us for a very long time. No one knows how long – no one can remember. If you saw a Silent, then the moment you looked away, you forgot they were ever there. The only way to fight them was to record memories of the Silence while you still had them. The Doctor's friends marked the number of sightings on their own bodies, because they knew they would forget.

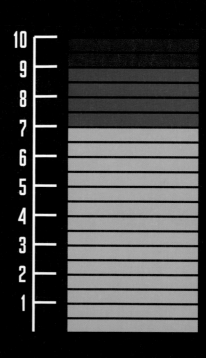

Fear Factor
9/10

Max Capricorn was a cyborg; only his head remained recognisably human. He was housed inside a wheeled, box-like life-support system. Founder of Max Capricorn Cruiseliners, Max Capricorn was voted off his own company board. He decided to get revenge by staging a meteoroid strike on his huge starship *Titanic* and then crashing it into Earth. The company would then be bankrupted by the claims for compensation.

Origin
Planet Sto

Doctors Encountered
Tenth

Description
Cyborg human in mobile life-support

But Capricorn hadn't counted on the Doctor being on board the *Titanic*. Surviving the meteoroid strike, the Doctor and other survivors, including the waitress Astrid Peth, discovered Capricorn's plan and tracked him down to a secret compartment on the ship. Capricorn was killed when Astrid used a forklift truck to push him into the ship's engines, sacrificing her own life in the process.

10
9
8
7
6
5
4
3
2
1

Fear Factor
5/10

Heavenly Host

The Heavenly Host were the helpful, informative assistants on the *Titanic* and other Max Capricorn star liners. They were designed to look like classical angels.

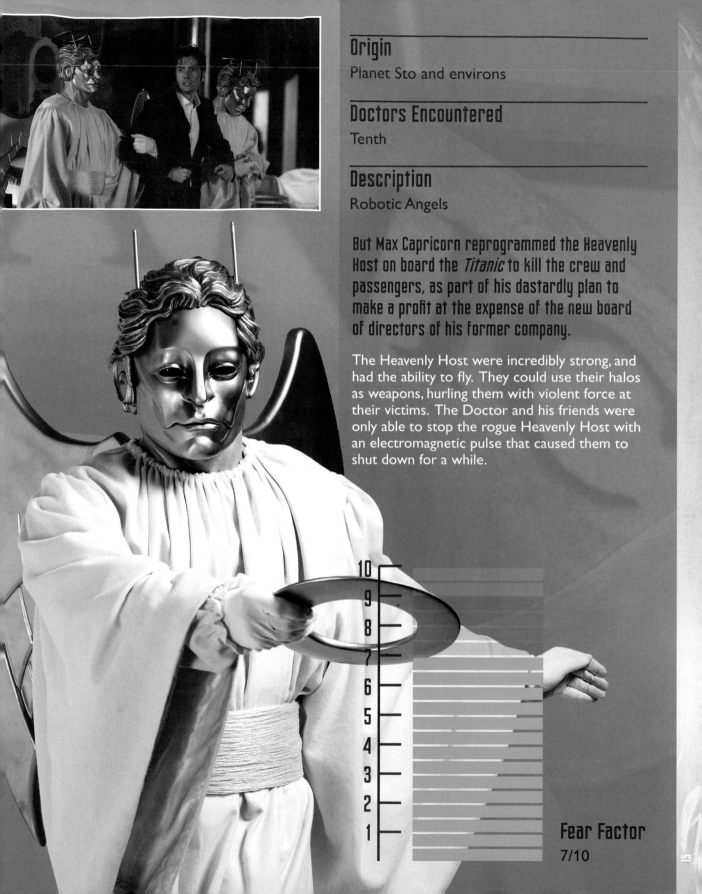

Origin

Planet Sto and environs

Doctors Encountered

Tenth

Description

Robotic Angels

But Max Capricorn reprogrammed the Heavenly Host on board the *Titanic* to kill the crew and passengers, as part of his dastardly plan to make a profit at the expense of the new board of directors of his former company.

The Heavenly Host were incredibly strong, and had the ability to fly. They could use their halos as weapons, hurling them with violent force at their victims. The Doctor and his friends were only able to stop the rogue Heavenly Host with an electromagnetic pulse that caused them to shut down for a while.

10
9
8
7
6
5
4
3
2
1

Fear Factor

7/10

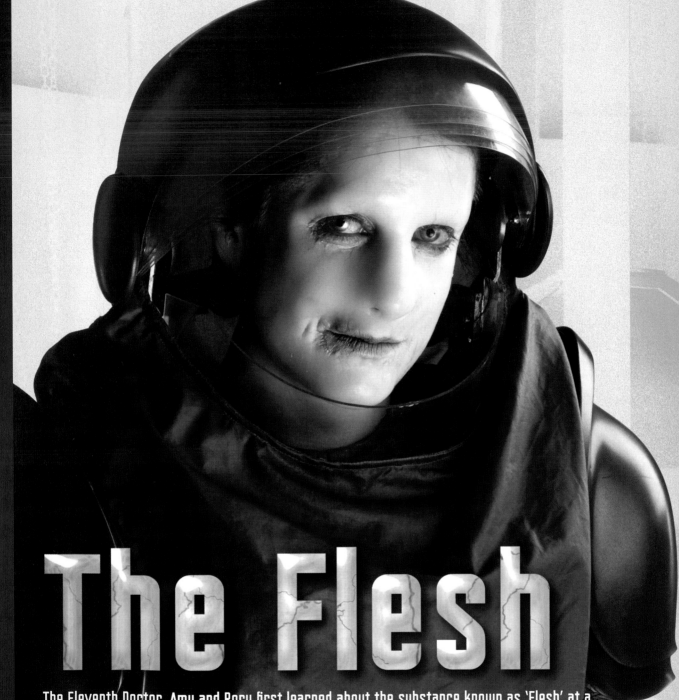

The Flesh

The Eleventh Doctor, Amy and Rory first learned about the substance known as 'Flesh' at a factory where acid was mined and refined. The human crewmembers were replaced with copies of themselves made from the Flesh – which could replicate their DNA, form and even memories. But these doppelgängers (or 'gangers' for short) could operate in the hazardous environment and the crew knew they would not be hurt or killed. If a ganger came to harm, they could simply create another while their own original body remained safe.

Origin

Planet Earth

Doctors Encountered

Eleventh

Description

Glutinous organic substance able to copy humans

But what the crew did not know was that after being primed with an electric charge, the Flesh could create gangers that were almost as human as the originals – and which resented being used as slaves by the human crew.

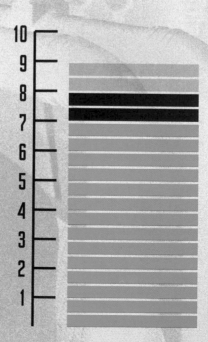

10
9
8
7
6
5
4
3
2
1

Fear Factor

8/10

PEG DOLLS

When Amy Pond and Rory Williams found themselves trapped in a strange house, they were attacked by the Peg Dolls – giant dolls apparently made from huge, old-fashioned clothes pegs.

In fact they were inside a doll's house, banished there by George, an alien Tenza child who desperately wanted to fit into his human family. George sent people who frightened him to the doll's house – including his neighbour Mrs Rossiter, landlord Mr Purcell, and eventually the Doctor and even George's own father, Alex. He released them when he realised that his family loved him and that he was safe.

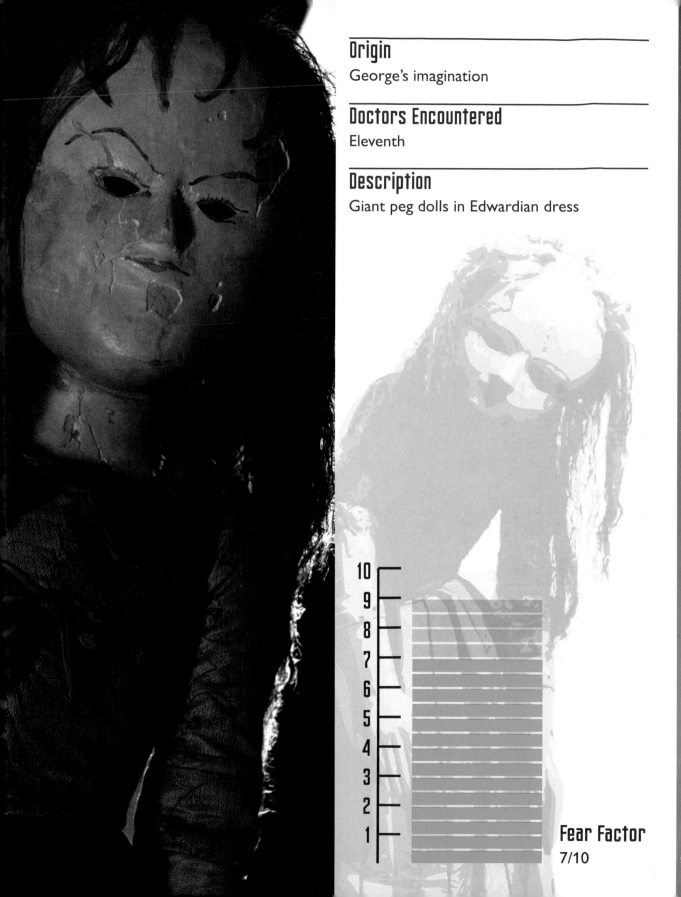

Origin

George's imagination

Doctors Encountered

Eleventh

Description

Giant peg dolls in Edwardian dress

10
9
8
7
6
5
4
3
2
1

Fear Factor
7/10

The Dream Lord

One of the greatest enemies of the Doctor doesn't actually exist. The Dream Lord was an illusion – just like the dream worlds he created. He became manifest when a speck of psychic pollen from the candle meadows of Karass don Slava fell into the TARDIS time rotor. When it was heated up it produced a dream-like state. The pollen is a mind parasite that feeds on everything dark in the host's mind – in this case, it produced the Dream Lord out of the darkness it found inside the Doctor's mind.

Origin

Illusion created by pollen

Doctors Encountered

Eleventh

Description

Apparently human

It is not clear if the alien Eknodines that the Doctor encountered in the dream world were 'real' aliens that appeared within the dream, or if they were entirely fictional – another part of the illusion. The creatures lived inside old people in Leadworth – the aliens' eyes appearing out of their mouths.

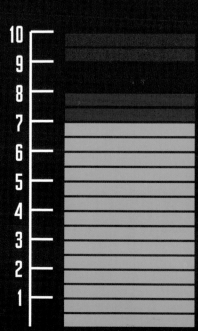

Fear Factor

8/10

The Krafayis are usually invisible. The creature encountered by the Doctor, Amy and the painter Vincent van Gogh was also blind, though it may have been injured. This may also explain why it killed several local villagers, apparently out of instinct or unbridled aggression – possibly it was afraid and in pain.

The Doctor was eventually able to identify the savage, invisible creature and cornered it in a church. Fighting an invisible enemy is never easy, but the Doctor was able to escape serious injury and the creature died. Vincent van Gogh could see the Krafayis, perhaps because of his own madness, or perhaps because he simply looked at the world in a different way to everyone else.

Origin
Unknown

Doctors Encountered
Eleventh

Description
Large, savage creature — usually invisible

10
9
8
7
6
5
4
3
2
1

Fear Factor
8/10

Smilers and Winders

The Smilers were information, assistance and teaching robots seated in booths on *Starship UK* in the twenty-ninth century. But part of their job was to preserve the ship's terrible secret and so they also kept the population from questioning the status quo. They could change from smiling to angry in a moment, their heads rotating to show a new expression.

The Smilers were maintained by the Winders – more sophisticated automata that acted as a security force on *Starship UK*. They wore a large key round their neck (hence their name), and their heads could also rotate to show the same grimacing, angry features as the Smilers.

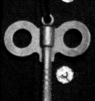

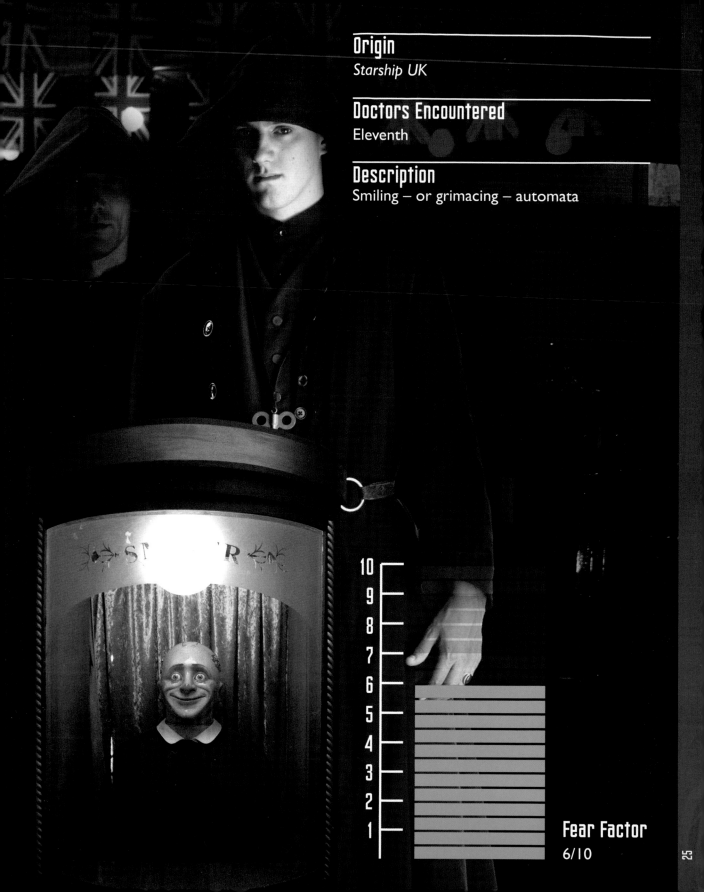

Origin
Starship UK

Doctors Encountered
Eleventh

Description
Smiling – or grimacing – automata

10
9
8
7
6
5
4
3
2
1

Fear Factor
6/10

Star Whale

The last of the great Star Whales came to Earth when the planet was being evacuated. It heard the sound of the children crying, and helped the people of Britain by carrying the enormous *Starship UK* into space on its back. The whole spaceship was embedded in the Star Whale, so that the creature powered all the systems and in effect became the engines of the ship.

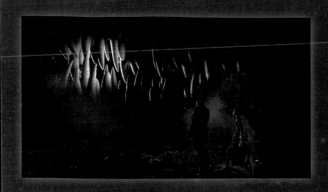

Origin
Deep space

Doctors Encountered
Eleventh

Description
Enormous space creature

But over the years, people forgot – and the government actively suppressed the memory of the Star Whale.

It was not until the Doctor and Amy arrived that the truth became widely known, and that the Star Whale was freed to decide if it wanted to continue with its task. Free of human control and the pain of being forced to power the ship, the Star Whale continued on its journey, taking *Starship UK* through space.

10
9
8
7
6
5
4
3
2
1

Fear Factor
4/10

Shark

When he visited Sardicktown, the Doctor found an environment where fish could actually live in the clouds above the planet. Occasionally, the fish descended to the surface of the planet when fog or mist became thick and hung low in the sky.

Most of the fish were harmless, attracted to the light from lamp-posts, for example. But larger, more dangerous fish also live in the fog, so Fish Warnings were given when the fog became too low and too thick.

The Doctor and young Kazran Sardick were attacked by a shark in Kazran's bedroom. They managed to save themselves with the Doctor's sonic screwdriver, but the shark was killed.

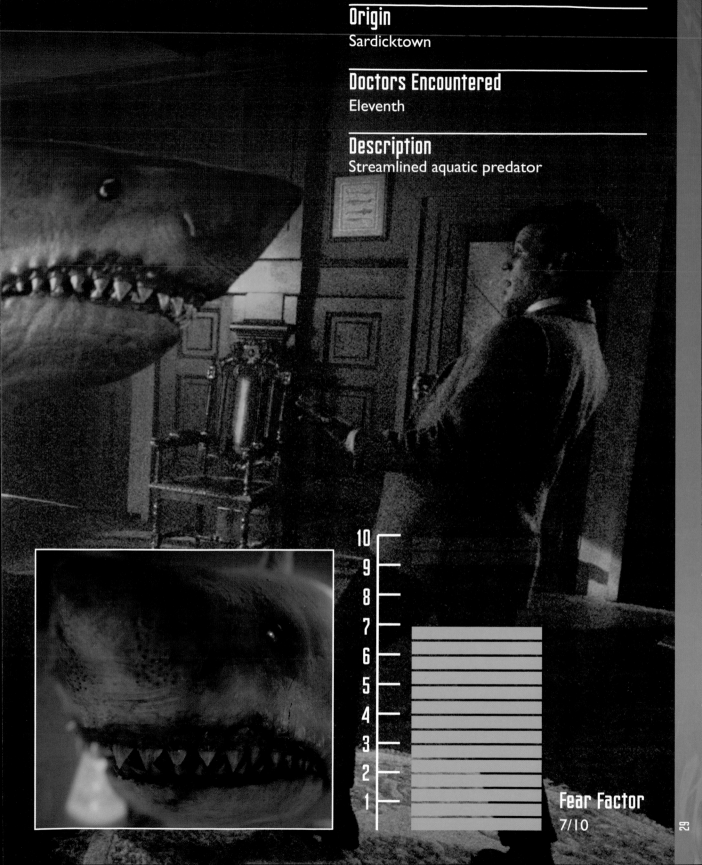

Origin
Sardicktown

Doctors Encountered
Eleventh

Description
Streamlined aquatic predator

10
9
8
7
6
5
4
3
2
1

Fear Factor
7/10

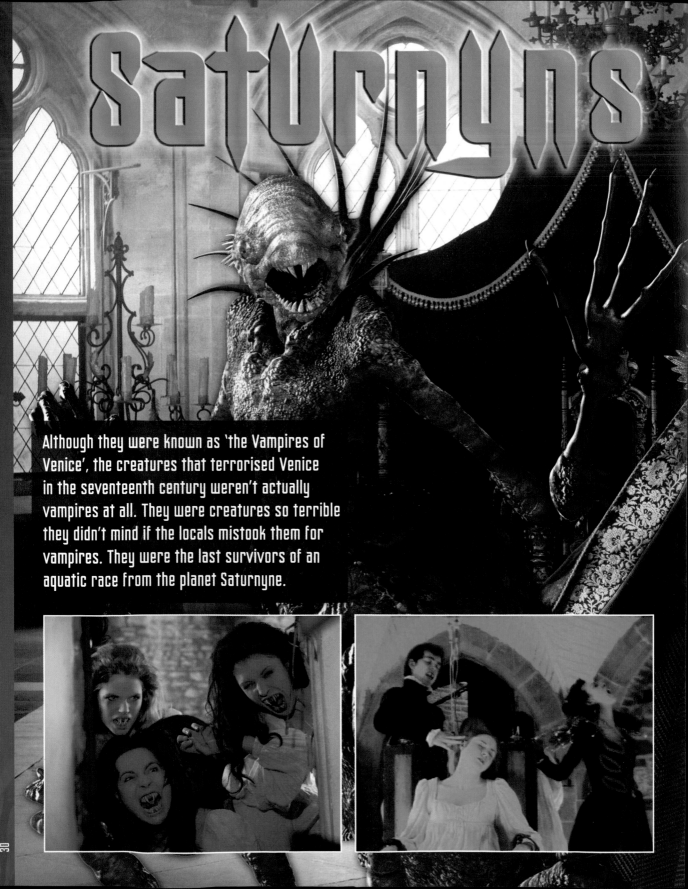

Saturnyns

Although they were known as 'the Vampires of Venice', the creatures that terrorised Venice in the seventeenth century weren't actually vampires at all. They were creatures so terrible they didn't mind if the locals mistook them for vampires. They were the last survivors of an aquatic race from the planet Saturnyne.

Origin
Planet Saturnyne

Doctors Encountered
Eleventh

Description
Upright, scaled aquatic creature

Only one female, Rosanna, and her male children survived the journey to Earth. But for Rosanna's race to continue to survive, she needed brides for her sons. So she devised a plan to turn young Venetian women into Saturnynian brides, and to sink Venice below the water to make it into an ideal habitat for her race.

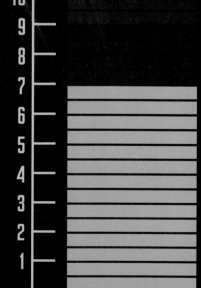

10
9
8
7
6
5
4
3
2
1

Fear Factor
7/10

Pilot Fish Santa Robots

'Pilot Fish' creatures scavenge in the wake of other predators. The Pilotfish Robots encountered by the Tenth Doctor initially came to Earth ahead of the attacking Sycorax. They were drawn to the residual energy left in the Doctor after his recent regeneration, and disguised themselves in festive attire to track him down.

Most appeared in Santa Claus outfits and masks, while one became a murderous Christmas Tree. Seeming to sense that Rose, Mickey and Jackie Tyler had been with the Doctor, they tried to eliminate them first.

The robots were later reprogrammed to serve the Empress of the Racnoss. They were destroyed when the Tenth Doctor destroyed the Empress.

Origin
Unknown

Doctors Encountered
Tenth

Description
Humanoid robots wearing Santa costumes and masks

10
9
8
7
6
5
4
3
2
1

Fear Factor
8/10

Racnoss

The Racnoss originally came from the so-called Dark Times, billions of years ago. The young Racnoss were born hungry and devoured everything – even whole planets. Because of this, the Fledgeling Empires went to war against the Racnoss and it was thought they had wiped them out.

But one Racnoss survived – the Empress of the Racnoss. Held in hibernation, she drifted in her Webstar spaceship to the very edge of space. When she finally awoke from her slumbers, she sought the last of her subjects. She found her unhatched offspring had escaped into the orbit of a new star – just as its solar system was forming. A new planet had formed round the Racnoss eggs – Earth. It was only the intervention of the Tenth Doctor, with the help of his new friend Donna Noble, that prevented the Racnoss children from hatching and devouring Earth.

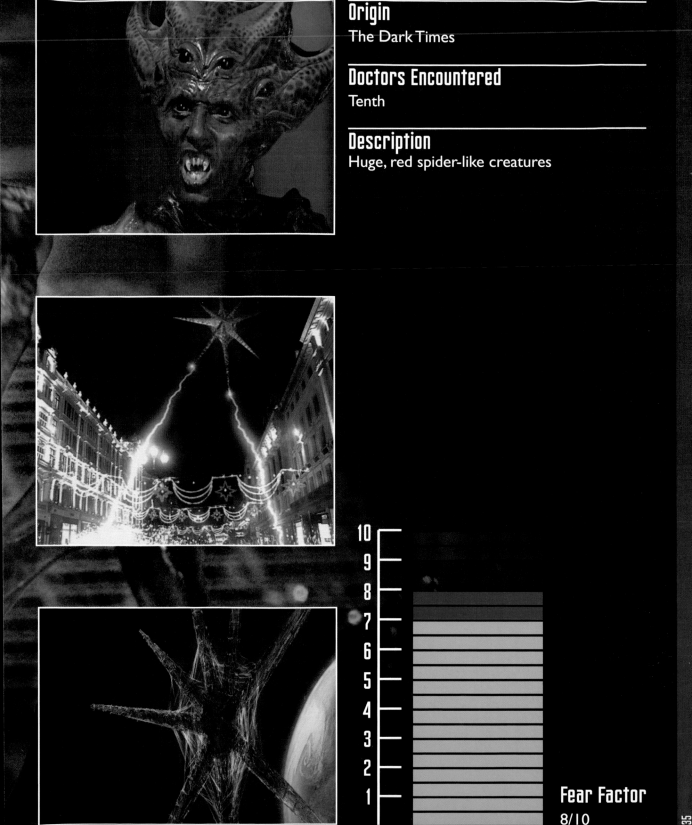

Origin
The Dark Times

Doctors Encountered
Tenth

Description
Huge, red spider-like creatures

10
9
8
7
6
5
4
3
2
1

Fear Factor
8/10

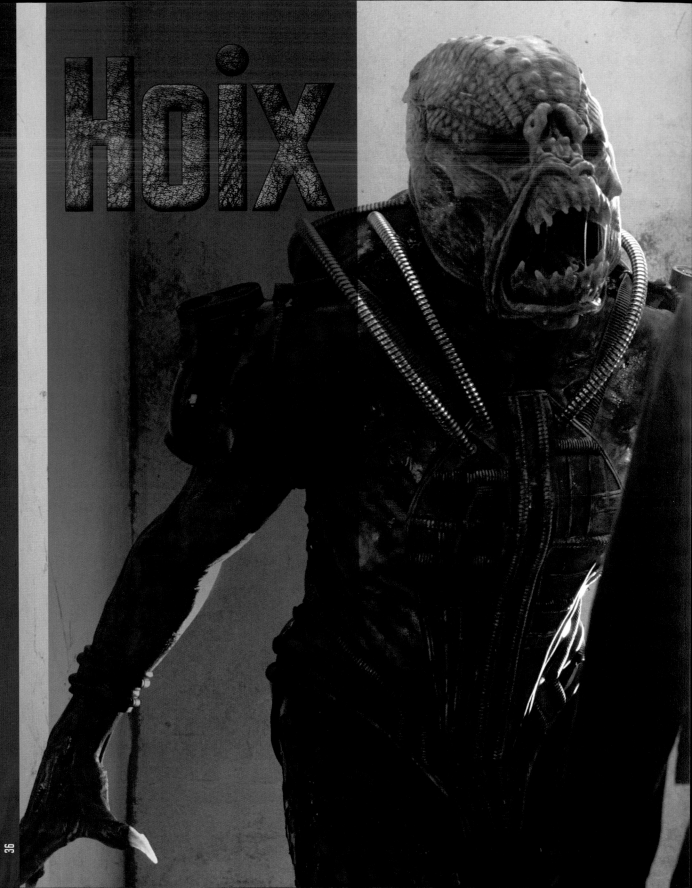

Hoix

Origin
Unknown

Doctors Encountered
Tenth, Eleventh

Description
Alien humanoid

The Hoix were involved in the alliance that imprisoned the Doctor in the Pandorica.

Little is known about the Hoix, though they were understood to be partial to pork chops. The Tenth Doctor and Rose battled against a Hoix in Woolwich. Elton Pope saw the Doctor and Rose trying to calm the Hoix by throwing the liquid contents of a red bucket over it. Elton ran off before seeing what happened, but he heard the TARDIS dematerialise – the Hoix, presumably, having been dealt with.

10
9
8
7
6
5
4
3
2
1

Fear Factor
5/10

Sycorax

An ancient race of warriors, the Sycorax conquered worlds and enslaved their inhabitants. They travelled in distinctive rock-formed spaceships and wore masks of bone-like material. Often, they would avoid direct confrontation with the places they conquered by tricking the leaders of the world into surrendering a proportion of their own people into slavery.

The Sycorax answered to a single leader, chosen by right of combat and strength. Their ships were more like ancient caves than technological equipment, and decorated with trophies of past Sycorax conquests. Their voices were brutally savage guttural growls and their native language was called Sycoraxic.

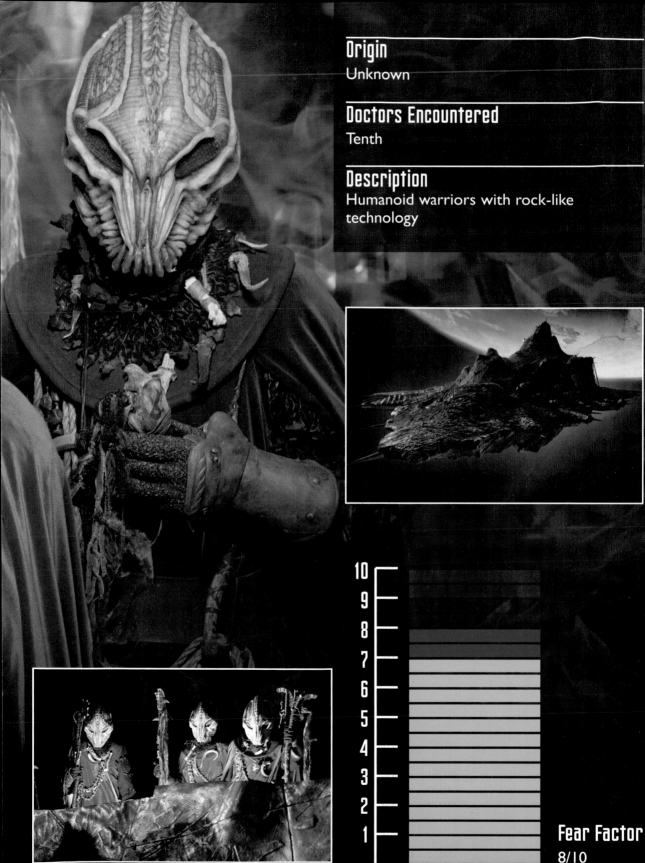

Origin
Unknown

Doctors Encountered
Tenth

Description
Humanoid warriors with rock-like technology

10
9
8
7
6
5
4
3
2
1

Fear Factor
8/10

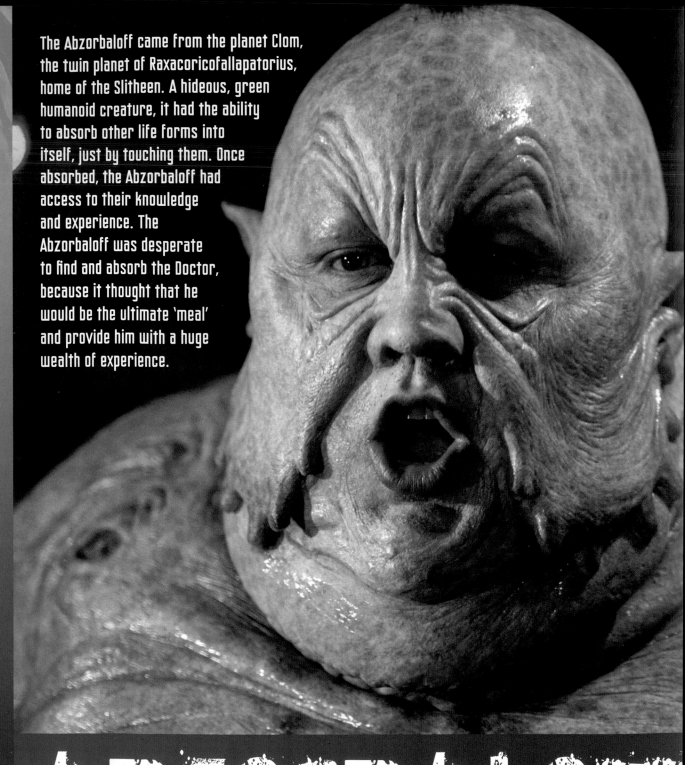

The Abzorbaloff came from the planet Clom, the twin planet of Raxacoricofallapatorius, home of the Slitheen. A hideous, green humanoid creature, it had the ability to absorb other life forms into itself, just by touching them. Once absorbed, the Abzorbaloff had access to their knowledge and experience. The Abzorbaloff was desperate to find and absorb the Doctor, because it thought that he would be the ultimate 'meal' and provide him with a huge wealth of experience.

ABZORBALOFF

Origin
Planet Clom

Doctors Encountered
Tenth

Description
Green humanoid with remnants of absorbed victims visible

For a while the victims of the Abzorbaloff were still visible – as faces embedded in its skin. They retained some individuality and could talk and even read the Abzorbaloff's thoughts. This was its downfall, because ultimately, the Abzorbaloff was destroyed by the combined will of its victims working together to pull it apart.

10
9
8
7
6
5
4
3
2
1

Fear Factor
6/10

Clockwork Robots

The clockwork-powered repair robots on the spaceship *Mme de Pompadour* were programmed to repair the ship using any components that they could find. When the ship was critically damaged in an ion storm, they carried out their programming, even though this meant taking body parts from the crew, and travelling in time to find Mme de Pompadour's head to replace the ship's damaged computer.

Searching for Reinette – the real Madame de Pompadour – in eighteenth century France, the clockwork robots disguised themselves in contemporary clothing and wigs, and wore ornate masks as if for a masked ball. Luckily the Tenth Doctor was able to rescue Reinette before the robots could remove her head.

Origin
Unknown

Doctors Encountered
Tenth

Description
Humanoid clockwork robots

Fear Factor
7/10

Prisoner Zero

Its real name is unknown, but the Atraxi imprisoned the entity they called Prisoner Zero. When Prisoner Zero escaped, they hunted across space for the criminal.

One of an interdimensional multiform species, Prisoner Zero could form a link with a living but dormant person, and then copy the shape of anyone or anything they dreamed about. In its natural form, Prisoner Zero was a large, gelatinous snake-like creature with sharp teeth.

After escaping through one of the cracks in the Universe caused by the TARDIS's later explosion, Prisoner Zero hid in Amy Pond's house. It blocked her perception of the room where it hid, and it was not until the Doctor came back years later that Prisoner Zero was discovered. By then the Atraxi had also tracked Prisoner Zero down.

Origin
Unknown

Doctors Encountered
Eleventh

Description
Multiform – native shape a large, gelatinous snake

10
9
8
7
6
5
4
3
2
1

Fear Factor
8/10

Atraxi

The Atraxi were one of the life forms that joined the alliance to imprison the Doctor in the Pandorica. Little else is known about them, except for the Prisoner Zero incident.

When Prisoner Zero escaped from an Atraxi prison through a crack in time, the Atraxi pursued it to Earth. Here they threatened to destroy the whole planet if Prisoner Zero was not surrendered to them. With the help of Amy and Rory, the Doctor was able to lead the Atraxi directly to Prisoner Zero. The Doctor then warned the Atraxi to leave Earth alone, and invoked Article 57 of the Shadow Proclamation.

Origin
Unknown

Doctors Encountered
Eleventh

Description
Large crystalline creatures with a huge single eye

10
9
8
7
6
5
4
3
2
1

Fear Factor
6/10

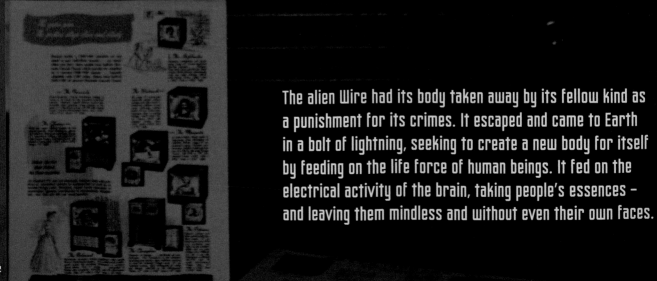

The Wire

The alien Wire had its body taken away by its fellow kind as a punishment for its crimes. It escaped and came to Earth in a bolt of lightning, seeking to create a new body for itself by feeding on the life force of human beings. It fed on the electrical activity of the brain, taking people's essences – and leaving them mindless and without even their own faces.

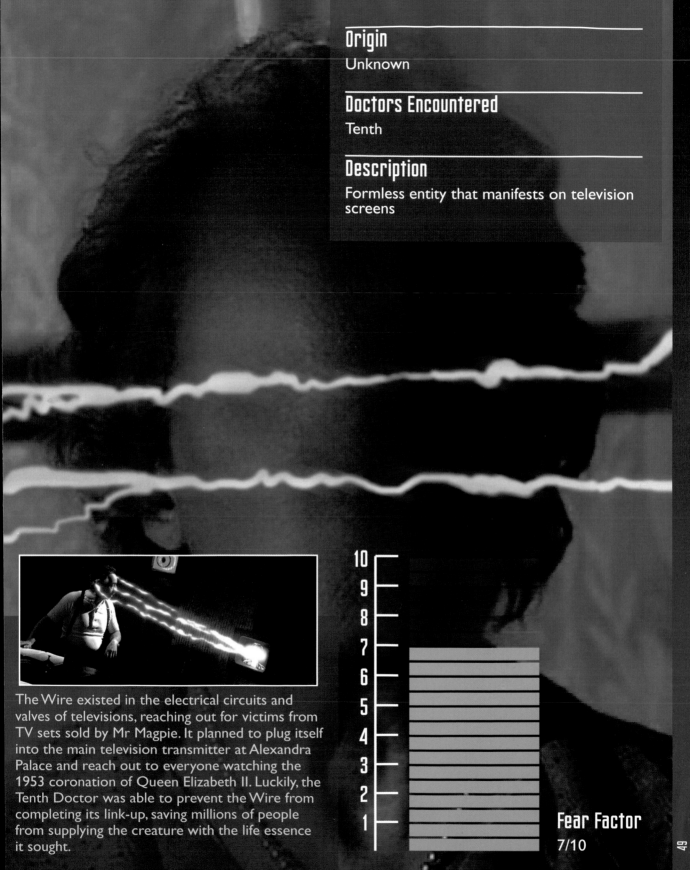

Origin
Unknown

Doctors Encountered
Tenth

Description
Formless entity that manifests on television screens

The Wire existed in the electrical circuits and valves of televisions, reaching out for victims from TV sets sold by Mr Magpie. It planned to plug itself into the main television transmitter at Alexandra Palace and reach out to everyone watching the 1953 coronation of Queen Elizabeth II. Luckily, the Tenth Doctor was able to prevent the Wire from completing its link-up, saving millions of people from supplying the creature with the life essence it sought.

10
9
8
7
6
5
4
3
2
1

Fear Factor
7/10

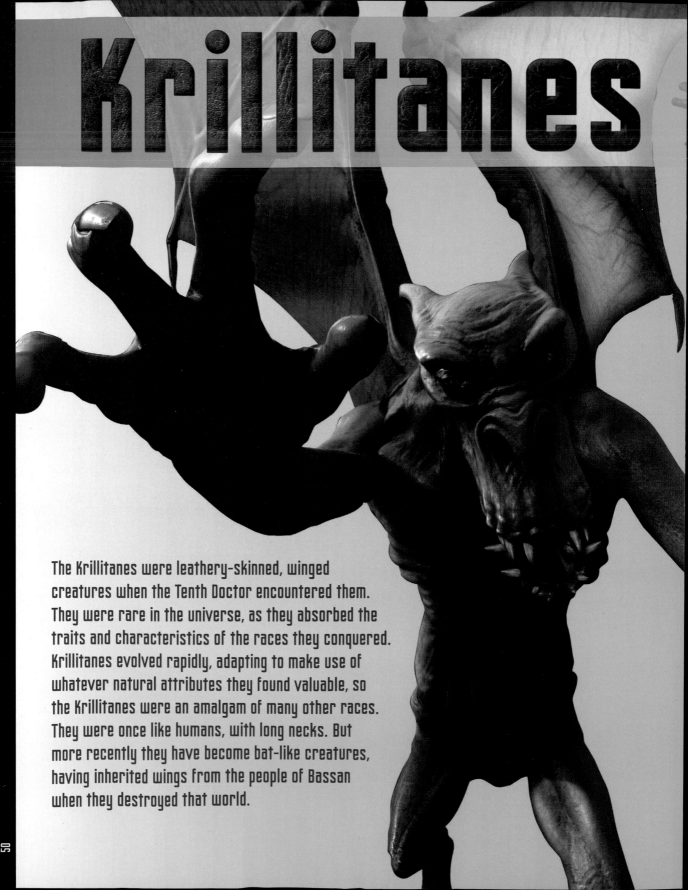

Krillitanes

The Krillitanes were leathery-skinned, winged creatures when the Tenth Doctor encountered them. They were rare in the universe, as they absorbed the traits and characteristics of the races they conquered. Krillitanes evolved rapidly, adapting to make use of whatever natural attributes they found valuable, so the Krillitanes were an amalgam of many other races. They were once like humans, with long necks. But more recently they have become bat-like creatures, having inherited wings from the people of Bassan when they destroyed that world.

Origin

Unknown

Doctors Encountered

Tenth

Description

Super-evolving creatures that secrete oil

The Krillitanes were able to disguise themselves and appear human using a simple morphic illusion. But the true Krillitane was not far below the surface – a vicious carnivore. The Doctor managed to defeat them with the help of Rose Tyler, Mickey Smith, Sarah Jane Smith and K-9, as the Krillitanes had evolved to a point where they were allergic to their own oil.

10
9
8
7
6
5
4
3
2
1

Fear Factor
8/10

Werewolf

In 1540, a spore or virus, or possibly the last *thought* of a powerful creature, crashed to Earth in the Glen of St Catherine in Scotland. Found and helped by the Brethren from the nearby monastery, it survived, grew, adapted and evolved slowly down the generations until it could take over a human Host and live within it. When the Host grew old and died, it moved to another – taking a child from each generation as its victim, carving out the child's soul and sitting in his heart.

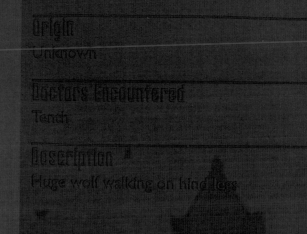

Origin
Unknown

Doctors Encountered
Tenth

Description
Huge wolf walking on hind legs

Drawing on the local legends and folklore, it mapped itself on to the creature at the centre of werewolf legends – a being that turns into a hideous wolf when the moon is full. It planned to take over Queen Victoria, but the Doctor was able to destroy the creature before it could carry out its plan.

Cybermen

Cybermen developed both in our own universe, and on a parallel world, where a man called John Lumic experimented with creating the next stage of human evolution – 'Human point 2'.

The main driving force of the Cybermen is the driving force of evolution itself – the need to survive. They pursue this at the cost of other life forms. The Doctor has battled against the Cybermen in almost all his incarnations ...

Origin
Mondas / Telos / Parallel Earth

Doctors Encountered
First, Second, Third, Fourth, Fifth, Sixth,
Seventh, Tenth, Eleventh

Description
Cybernetically enhanced humans

The Cybermen were once human, like us. But
using advanced technology they replaced
their limbs and organs with plastic and metal.
Only their brains remained, but with all the
emotions removed. The result was a race of
pitiless monsters that will do whatever they
have to in order to survive.

10
9
8
7
6
5
4
3
2
1

Fear Factor
9/10

Cybermats

The Cybermats were rodent-like cybernetic creatures created by the Cybermen. They were possibly converted from (or using the brain of) a small animal such as a rat or a cat. Cybermats performed limited – but deadly – functions.

Origin
Planet Telos

Doctors Encountered
Second, Fourth

Description
Cybernetic life form

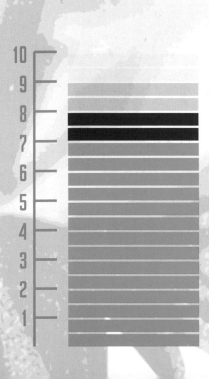

One type of Cybermat had eyes, antennae and a segmented tail. Underneath they moved on rows of filaments, and they had what seemed to be rows of teeth. They could home in on human brainwaves to attack. A variation of this type, which attacked the Wheel in Space, had spines down their back, no antennae and solid, unfacetted eyes.

The Cybermats used by the Cybermen to infiltrate Nerva Beacon and infect its crew with a deadly virus were longer, with segmented bodies and a small red sensor at the front. The Fourth Doctor adapted one of these Cybermats to attack the Cybermen with gold dust.

10
9
8
7
6
5
4
3
2
1

Fear Factor
8/10

The highest rank of Cyberman is the Cyber Controller. There is only one Controller at any given time, in overall charge of all Cyber operations. The Cyber Controller's design has changed through the generations, but generally he has an enlarged helmet housing a super-enhanced brain.

Origin
Planets Mondas, Telos and Parallel Earth

Doctors Encountered
Second, Sixth, Tenth

Description
Leader Cyberman with enlarged brain

CYBER CONTROLLER

The Second Doctor encountered the Cyber Controller that was awakened from the tombs of the Cybermen on their planet Telos. The Sixth Doctor did battle with another Cyber Controller on the same planet. The Cyber Controller that the Tenth Doctor encountered was the cybernised form of John Lumic, who created the Cybermen on a parallel version of Earth.

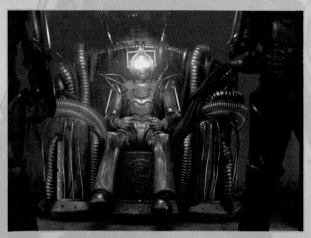

10
9
8
7
6
5
4
3
2
1

Fear Factor
9/10

Cybershade

In London, on Christmas Eve in 1851, the Doctor encountered a new type of Cyberman: the Cybershade. A large, dark, shaggy creature enhanced with Cyber head and hands, the Cybershades were more animal than Cyberman.

The Cybershades were agile, but deadly, and often used for reconnaissance as they were less conspicuous than the Cybermen in Victorian London. They could run, climb, jump, but were not equipped to administer lethal electric shocks, like normal Cybermen. They seemed to be totally subservient to their Cyberman masters, with no free will of their own, just the remnants of animal instinct and aggression.

Origin
Victorian London

Doctors Encountered
Tenth

Description
Savage, Cyber-enhanced creature

Fear Factor

6/10

CyberKing

The so-called CyberKing was actually a Dreadnought-class Cybership, complete with a Cyber Conversion and production Factory on board – ready to convert millions of humans into a new race of Cybermen. It was created by the Cybermen stranded in Victorian London in 1851, using slave labour and local materials and technology, rising from beneath the Thames to attack.

The CyberKing was controlled by the mental force of the adapted form of Miss Hartigan. Impressed with her cold-hearted ambition and ruthlessness, the Cybermen had decided she would be their supreme leader. But after being partly-converted into a Cyberman, she retained some of her original human emotions and her ambition, so her imagination was able to override the Cyber technology and destroy it.

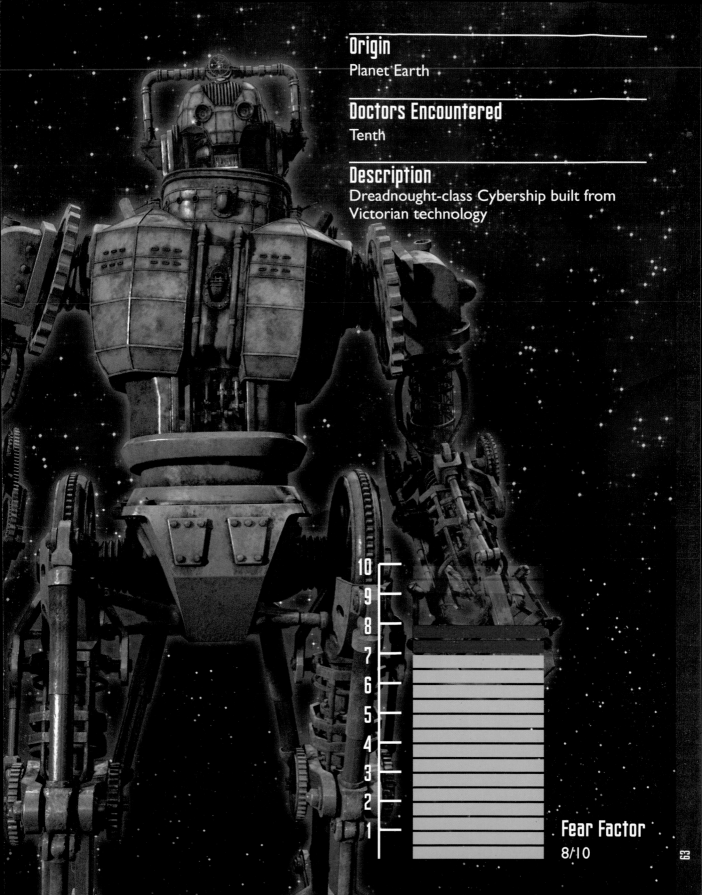

Origin
Planet Earth

Doctors Encountered
Tenth

Description
Dreadnought-class Cybership built from Victorian technology

10
9
8
7
6
5
4
3
2
1

Fear Factor
8/10

Plasmavore Florence

The Tenth Doctor and Martha encountered a Plasmavore that had disguised itself as an old lady called Florence. She was being hunted by the Judoon, and had hidden out at the Royal Hope Hospital. In fact, she was a blood-sucking vampire who had already murdered the Child Princess of Padrivole Regency Nine.

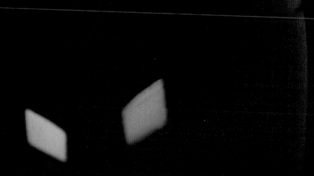

Origin
Unknown

Doctors Encountered
Tenth

Description
Disguised as an inoffensive old lady

Depending on blood to survive, the Plasmavore was able to assimilate an alien's biological make-up through its blood, and so escape being identified by the Judoon when they scanned for non-human life forms. She carried her own drinking straw ready to take blood from whoever was available – the richer and more salty and fatty the blood, the better.

The Plasmavore was protected by two basic slave drones that looked just like motorcycle couriers, complete with black leather uniforms and crash helmets. In fact, these 'Slabs' were made of solid leather imbued with simple life and the ability to obey orders from the Plasmavore.

10
9
8
7
6
5
4
3
2
1

Fear Factor
8/10

Judoon

The Judoon are an intergalactic mercenary police force for hire. They were dedicated to upholding law and order and worked for other races and authorities, including the Shadow Proclamation, to provide security and policing services. Efficient and ruthless, the Judoon had little interest in other races unless they broke the law. Anyone who stood in their way could be found guilty of obstruction or assault and executed.

Hugely powerful and not unlike large upright rhinoceroses, the Judoon arrived in massive upright spaceships like tall tower blocks. They could only enforce Galactic Law where specifically invited or on neutral territory, and they were a part of the alliance that imprisoned the Doctor in the Pandorica.

Origin
Unknown

Doctors Encountered
Tenth, Eleventh

Description
Humanoid rhinocerid

10
9
8
7
6
5
4
3
2
1

Fear Factor
7/10

Long ago, the Carrionites developed a science that was based on words instead of numbers. While humanity followed the mathematical route, developing formulae and equations to try to explain and shape the universe, the Carrionites pursued a different path. The nature of their science makes the Carrionites seem like witches, chanting spells and using magic.

But the ancient Eternals found the spell – the right word – to banish the Carrionites into Deep Darkness. It was thought they could never return. But the death of Shakespeare's young son, Hamnet, released such grief in the great playwright that this conjured up three Carrionites in Elizabethan London. They used their 'magic' to have Shakespeare's words release all the Carrionites to feed on the world . . . But with Shakespeare's help, the Tenth Doctor and Martha were able to banish them back into the Deep Darkness.

Origin
The Rexel Planetary Configuration

Doctors Encountered
Tenth

Description
Ethereal hags that can disguise their form

10
9
8
7
6
5
4
3
2
1

Fear Factor
7/10

Lazarus Creature

Professor Richard Lazarus planned to use his Genetic Manipulation Device to change what it meant to be human – to renew himself and make himself younger. But the process damaged his DNA, bringing to the surface a series of molecules that should have remained dormant. The result was that Lazarus turned into a huge, primordial arthropod creature that needed to draw the life energy from other people in order to survive.

After it rampaged through the LazLabs complex, the Tenth Doctor managed to lure the creature into Southwark Cathedral, where it was killed. In death, the creature reverted to the form of Professor Lazarus.

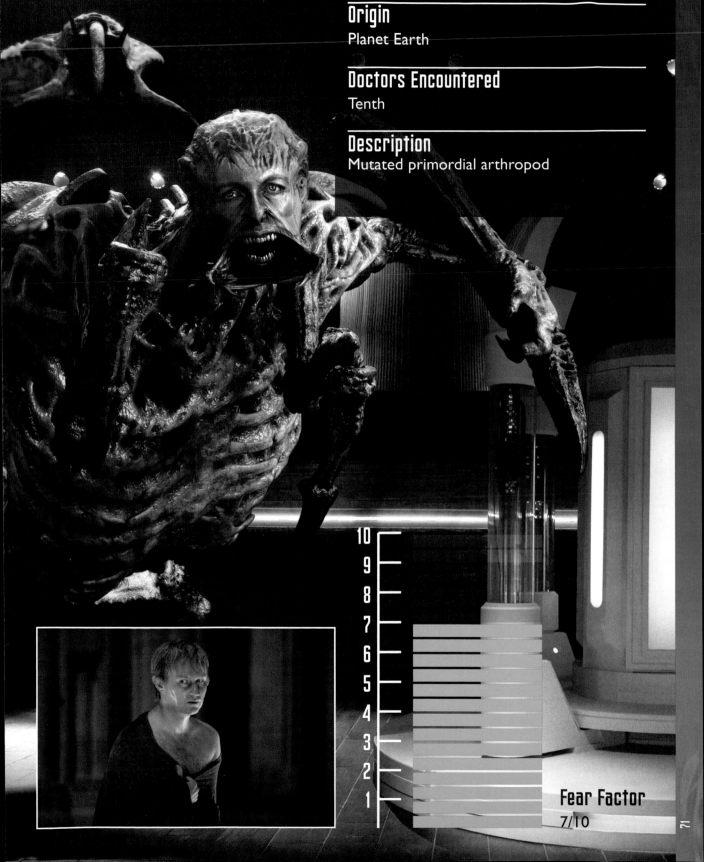

Origin
Planet Earth

Doctors Encountered
Tenth

Description
Mutated primordial arthropod

10
9
8
7
6
5
4
3
2
1

Fear Factor
7/10

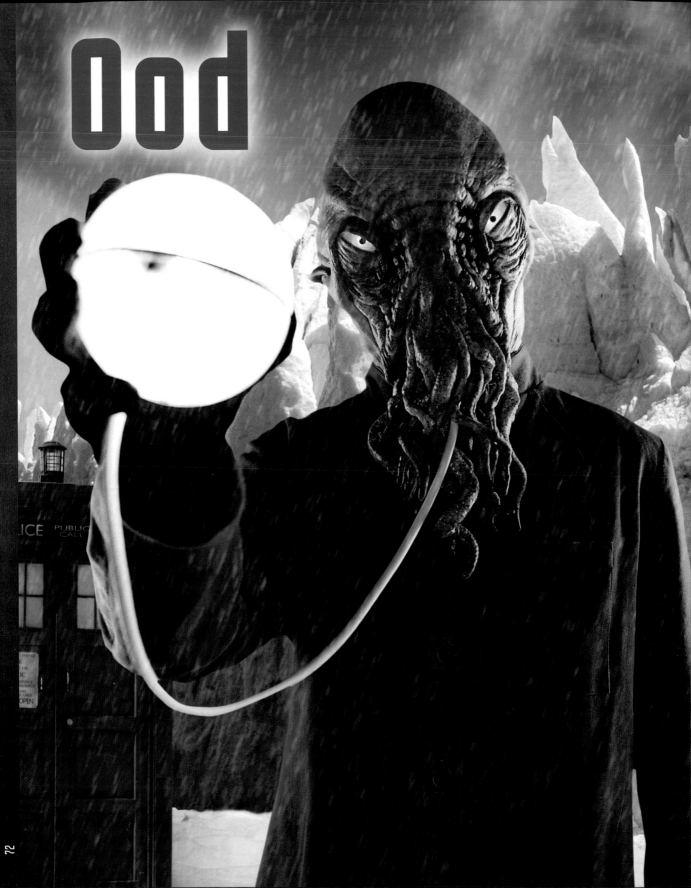

Ood

Origin

The Ood Sphere

Doctors Encountered

Tenth, Eleventh

Description

Humanoids with distinctive fronds in place of mouths

Because they were telepathic, the Ood could be influenced by other mental powers – like those used by the Beast. When they were dangerously possessed, the Oods" eyes glowed red ...

...d apparently existed to ...rvants to Mankind. They ...s a basic slave race and ...ined away and died. ...mans believed they were ...ould not be given orders ...es 'Friends of the Ood.'

...d Donna discovered, the ...re right. In their natural ...n intelligent and proactive. ...shared brain. But they ...d exploited and it was up ...em free.

10
9
8
7
6
5
4
3
2
1

Fear Factor
7/10

The Beast

At a time before time itself even existed, there was the Beast. Feared and deadly, it became the template for every representation of evil that followed, right across the universe. The Tenth Doctor speculated that the devil legends of Earth, Draconia, Velconsadine, Damos and even the Kaled God of War might stem originally from the Beast.

But despite its mighty power, the Beast was defeated and imprisoned on an isolated planet circling a black hole. The ancient people that captured the Beast did not kill it, but bound it to the core of the planet. They made sure that the planet itself circled the black hole – and that if the Beast ever escaped, it would be sucked in, destroying their ancient prisoner.

When the humans of Santuary Base 6 arrived on the so-called Impossible Planet, together with their telepathic Ood servants, the Beast saw a way, finally, to escape . . .

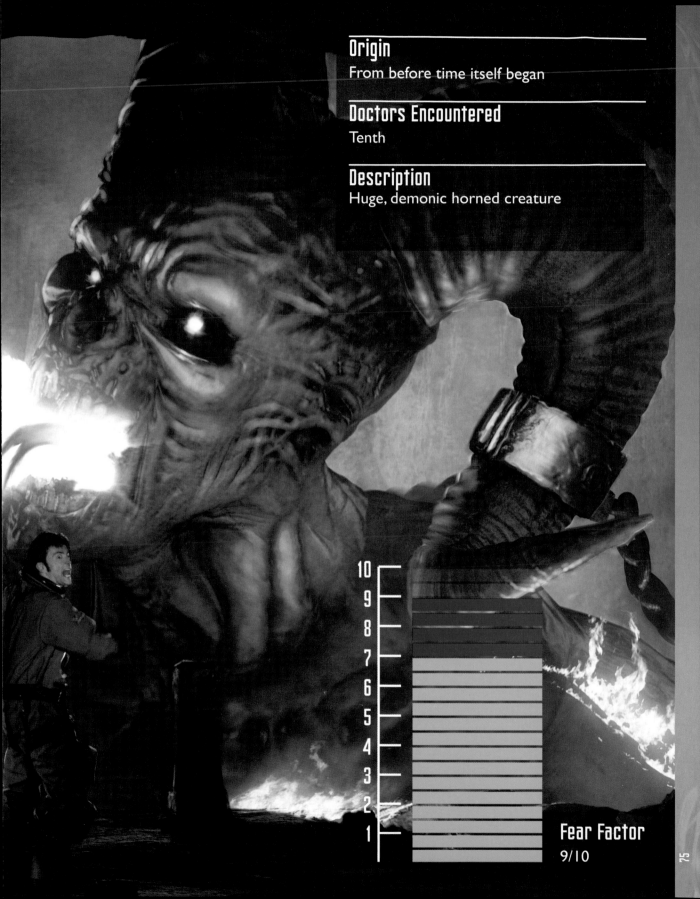

Origin
From before time itself began

Doctors Encountered
Tenth

Description
Huge, demonic horned creature

10
9
8
7
6
5
4
3
2
1

Fear Factor
9/10

Adipose Children

Adipose Industries claimed to market a revolutionary new diet pill. But in fact, the excess fat of anyone taking the capsule was ejected from the body as an infant Adipose creature.

The company was run by Miss Foster, who was actually Matron Cofelia, working for the Adiposian Royal Family. The ultimate end of the process would kill the 'donors', as the Adipose could also convert the whole human body – bone, organs, hair – into Adipose material.

Origin
Offspring of the Adiposian Royal Family

Doctors Encountered
Tenth

Description
Small creatures composed of fat, with eyes and a fang

A million of the Adipose were created when Miss Foster was forced to activate her full program early, when the Doctor and Donna Noble got involved. They stopped her plans, and the Adipose children already produced were rescued and taken into care by the Shadow Proclamation.

10
9
8
7
6
5
4
3
2
1

Fear Factor
3/10

Vespiform

In their natural form, the ancient and wise Vespiforms from the hives of the Silfrax Galaxy resembled giant wasps – complete with sting. Little is known about these creatures, but they could change their shape to resemble other life forms.

The only recorded instance of a Vespiform visiting Earth was in 1885, when it arrived in a blaze of purple fire. The Vespiform took the form of a human male called 'Christopher' in order to learn about the human race. Years later, the Tenth Doctor and Donna encountered the Vespiform's son – and managed to halt its murderous rampage with the help of crime writer Agatha Christie.

Origin
Silfrax Galaxy

Doctors Encountered
Tenth

Description
Giant wasps

Fear Factor
7/10

Sontarans

The Sontarans are a race dedicated to – and bred for – total war. They have been fighting the Rutan Host for millennia. They will attack anyone who gets in their way, or invade any planet which they think can give them a strategic advantage. They even tried to invade Gallifrey, the planet of the Time Lords.

Their home world Sontar is a planet with high gravity, which may explain the Sontarans' stunted appearance. They reproduce by cloning – at a rate of a million every four minutes in great muster parades. Being clones, all Sontarans are identical.

Despite their ruthlessness and brutality, the Sontarans have a keen sense of honour. They even see their greatest weakness as a strength because of this – a Sontaran can only be stunned by a blow to the probic vent, a small hole at the back of the neck. The Sontarans believe this means they must always face their enemies.

Origin
Planet Sontar

Doctors Encountered
Second, Third, Fourth, Sixth, Tenth, Eleventh

Description
Stocky humanoids in space armour with domed helmets

10
9
8
7
6
5
4
3
2
1

Fear Factor
8/10

Hath

An amphibious race, the Hath depended on oxygenated liquid to breathe. They could only survive out of water using special breathing equipment. Communication between humans and Hath was difficult, as the Hath 'voices' were filtered through the liquid and emerged as bubbles and gurgles.

Origin
Unknown

Doctors Encountered
Tenth

Description
Aquatic bipedal lifeform

A joint team of humans and Hath was sent to the colony planet of Messaline to clear out the old mining towns and adapt the ecosystem with a standard PT306 system. But the two races fell out and a conflict started – then escalated into war. Each side made use of recalibrated Progenation Machines to 'breed' new troops. Soon a war that had in fact lasted only days had claimed the lives of generations of Hath and humans.

10
9
8
7
6
5
4
3
2
1

Fear Factor
6/10

Stingrays

Origin
Unknown

Doctors Encountered
Tenth

Description
Huge flying creatures, similar to rays

The creatures swarmed in their billions and ate anything and everything, reducing it to sand. They ate metal, extruding it into their exoskeleton — so that they had metal bones. They flew at such a tremendous speed as they encircled the worlds they ravaged, that they opened a wormhole to take them to their next feeding ground — another planet. Their metal exoskeletons enabled them to survive the journey through the wormholes.

When these creatures came through a wormhole to attack Earth, UNIT referred to them as 'Stingrays'. But the huge, airborne creatures that devastated San Helios and many other worlds, turning them to barren deserts, bear only a superficial resemblance to real stingrays.

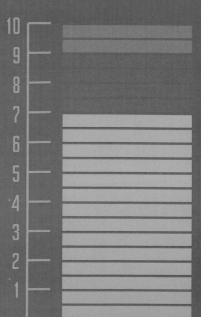

Fear Factor
7/10

Tritovores

The Tritovores were an insectoid race from the Scorpion Nebula that resembled giant, humanoid flies. They were a technologically advanced species, and had well-developed space flight, based on Crystal Nucl power. The Tritovores traded with other races and planets for the waste products which they fed on.

Communicating in their own chirping speech, the Tritovores could translate other alien languages so they could understand them. But the technology was not two-way, so it was difficult for others to understand the Tritovores. The Doctor met two Tritovores after their ship crashed on the planet San Helios — but both were killed by the alien 'stingrays' that turned the once highly developed planet to a barren desert.

Origin
The Scorpion Nebula

Doctors Encountered
Tenth

Description
Humanoid insectoids

10
9
8
7
6
5
4
3
2
1

Fear Factor
6/10

Vashta Nerada

The Vashta Nerada – also known as the Piranhas of the Air, or the Shadows that Eat the Flesh – was a swarm of *darkness* itself. The Vashta Nerada hatched from spores gathered in living wood, becoming a swarm in minutes. The spores could survive inside the wood when the tree died – which meant they could live in paper made from the wood pulp. They could live inside books . . .

They could hide in any shadow or any patch of darkness. They could *be* any shadow or patch of darkness. If someone had more than one shadow, then it's possible the Vashta Nerada had already claimed them… They could tear the flesh from a living being in an instant, and animate the remaining husk of a body.

Origin
Forests

Doctors Encountered
Tenth

Description
Shadow creatures

10
9
8
7
6
5
4
3
2
1

Fear Factor
9/10

Time Beetle

Little is known about these creatures. The one that changed Donna's life was a giant beetle that attached itself to her back. It sat there, sapping the time energy, occasionally glimpsed by others.

The Time Beetle was able to change time itself by manipulating the choices its victims made as they lived out their lives. Usually the resulting changes were so slight, and so tiny that they were barely noticeable. But in Donna's case, the small change in her life had catastrophic consequences...

In Donna's changed life, she never met the Doctor – so he died defeating the Empress of the Racnoss. Without the Doctor, other events took different courses and Donna's life became very different. With the help of Rose Tyler and UNIT, Donna was able to go back and reset things so that time again followed its proper course.

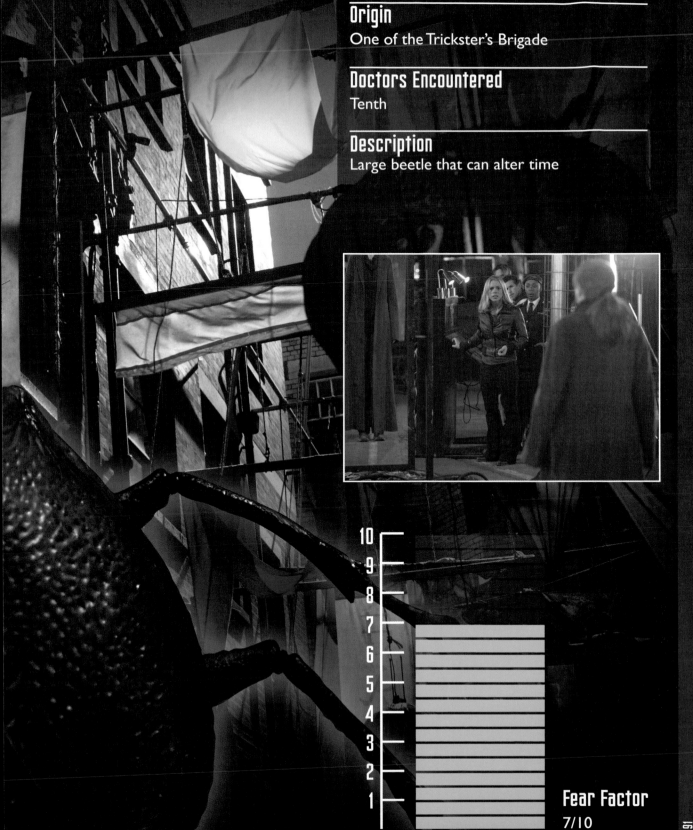

Origin
One of the Trickster's Brigade

Doctors Encountered
Tenth

Description
Large beetle that can alter time

Fear Factor
7/10

Midnight Entity

Very little is known about the strange entity that attacked the tourists on a Crusader 50 vehicle en route from the Leisure Palace to the fabled Sapphire Waterfall on the planet Midnight.

The planet is uninhabitable, bathed in lethal X-tonic sunlight that can vaporise a person in seconds. But something was out there, living on the surface. It managed to get inside the vehicle, and took over Sky Silvestry – one of the passengers. Possessed by the entity, she repeated whatever was said to her, eventually speaking at the same time as other people, and saying the same thing.

Realising the Tenth Doctor was the greatest threat, the entity stole his voice completely – so that he had to repeat what she said. With most of the passengers believing the Doctor was the real threat, the Midnight Entity was destroyed by the tour Hostess – who ejected herself and Sky out of the vehicle to be vaporised in the X-tonic sunlight.

Planet Midnight

Doctors Encountered

Tenth

Description

Unknown

10
9
9
8
8
7
7
6
6
5
5
4
4
3
3
2
2

Fear Factor
9/10

The Flood

Origin
Planet Mars

Doctors Encountered
Tenth

Description
Parasitic water, and the people it infects

On Mars, the Doctor faced a terrifying creature that lived in water and possessed anyone who came into contact with that water. They mutated into creatures with cracked skin, constantly dripping and running with water – and infecting anyone else they touched. A single drop of water was enough to infect anyone with the Flood.

The creature took over the crew of Bowie Base One and planned to travel back to Earth and infect the water supply there. But with the help of a menial robot, Gadget, the Doctor was able to rescue some of the crew before the base was completely destroyed in an explosion.

Fear Factor
9/10

Homo Reptilia

An ancient race, the Earth Reptiles – or Silurians as they are also known – lived on Earth long before the human race evolved. Threatened with catastrophe, the creatures retreated to shelters deep underground where they went into hibernation. Most of them have never woken up. But those who have, have found Earth now inhabited by the descendents of the primitive ape creatures from their own prehistoric time – the human race.

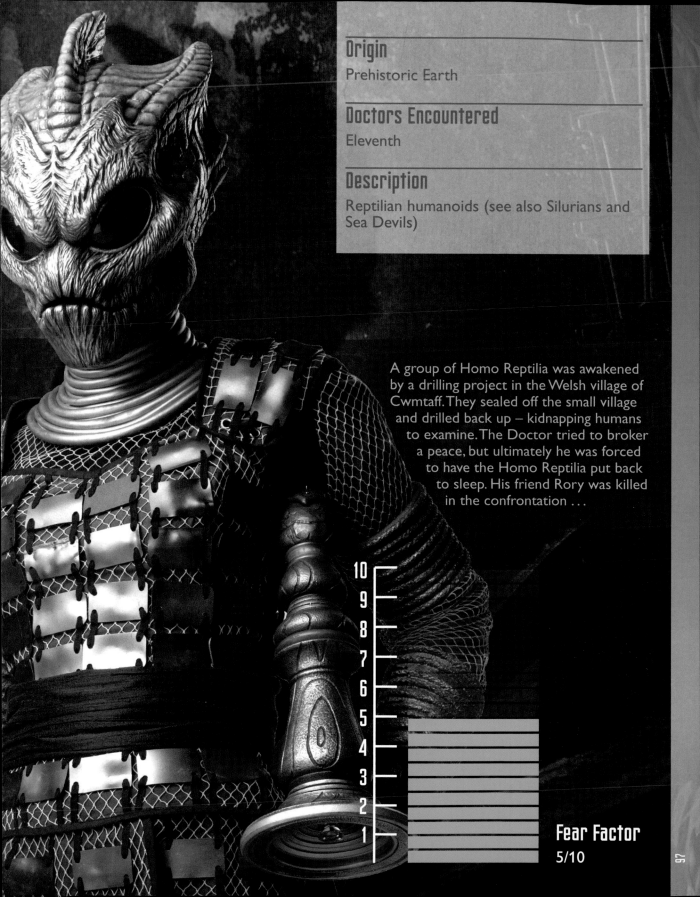

Origin

Prehistoric Earth

Doctors Encountered

Eleventh

Description

Reptilian humanoids (see also Silurians and Sea Devils)

A group of Homo Reptilia was awakened by a drilling project in the Welsh village of Cwmtaff. They sealed off the small village and drilled back up – kidnapping humans to examine. The Doctor tried to broker a peace, but ultimately he was forced to have the Homo Reptilia put back to sleep. His friend Rory was killed in the confrontation . . .

Fear Factor

5/10

Sea Devils

Underwater 'cousins' of the Silurians, the so-called Sea Devils are another form of Homo Reptilia that went into hibernation in prehistory to avoid being destroyed in a great catastrophe.

A group of Sea Devils was awakened by renovation work on an old sea fort, and the Master plotted with them to destroy humanity and reclaim Earth for themselves. Unable to broker a peace, the Third Doctor was able to defeat the Sea Devils with the help of the Royal Navy.

The Fifth Doctor encountered a combined force of Sea Devils and Silurians who attacked an underwater military base. Again, the Doctor desperately tried to negotiate a peaceful settlement, and again he was unsuccessful and the Sea Devils and Silurians – as well as the crew of the base – were all killed.

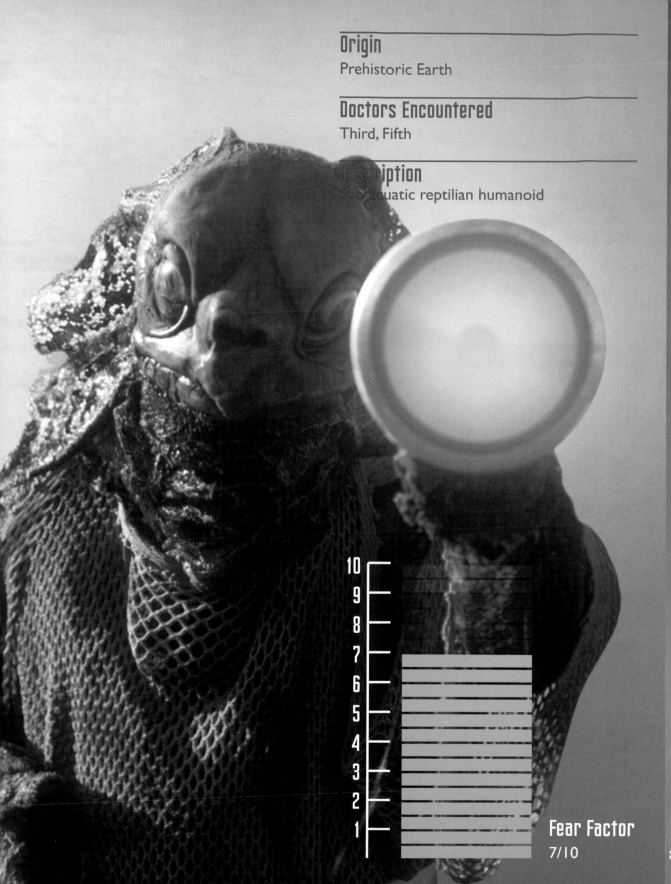

Origin
Prehistoric Earth

Doctors Encountered
Third, Fifth

Description
Subaquatic reptilian humanoid

10
9
8
7
6
5
4
3
2
1

Fear Factor
7/10

Silurians

Millions of years ago, when the creatures that would become humans were merely apes, Earth was inhabited by intelligent reptiles. But when a small planet was detected approaching Earth, they thought it would draw away the atmosphere and create a global catastrophe. To avoid this, they built huge hibernation chambers, where they slept through the crisis. They would be awakened when the atmosphere returned.

But the small planet never drew away the atmosphere, and so the reptiles never woke. Instead the planet was captured by Earth's gravity and became the Moon. The various groups of reptile that have awoken since – called Silurians and Sea Devils by the people who first encountered them – think of Earth as their own planet, and see humans as upstart apes to be destroyed.

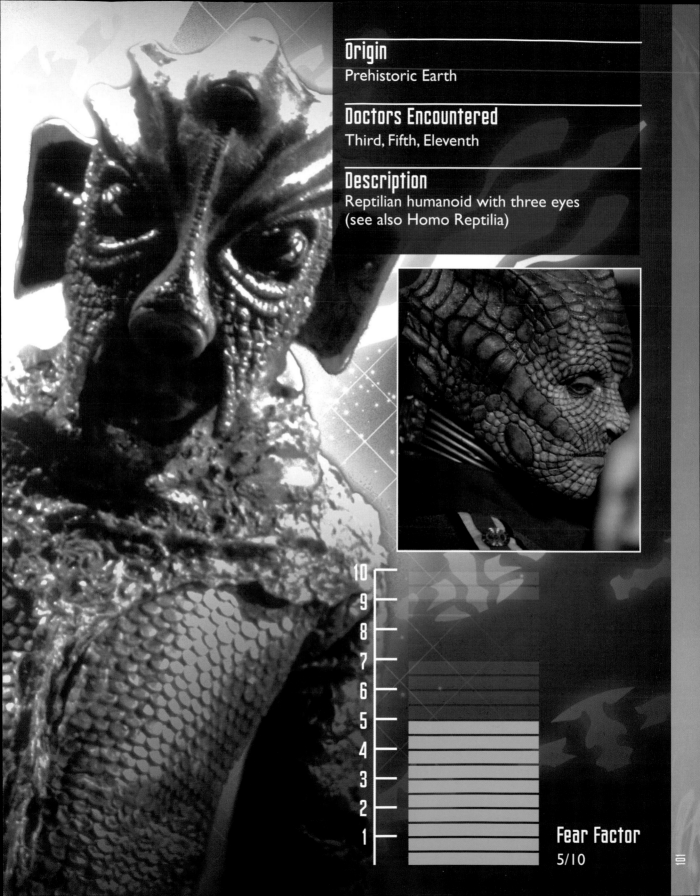

Origin
Prehistoric Earth

Doctors Encountered
Third, Fifth, Eleventh

Description
Reptilian humanoid with three eyes
(see also Homo Reptilia)

Fear Factor
5/10

Gelth

The Ninth Doctor and Rose Tyler encountered the Gelth in Cardiff in the nineteenth century, when they also met the writer Charles Dickens. The Gelth were ethereal, bodiless creatures that pretended to need help. For a while, even the Doctor was taken in. But then he realised the Gelth wanted to possess the bodies of everyone on Earth.

Essentially gaseous creatures, in this world the Gelth 'lived' in the gas pipes – the environment most suited to them. They were able to possess and reanimate the bodies of dead people – turning them into Gelth-controlled zombies. The Doctor eventually destroyed the bridge between our world and the dimension where the Gelth existed.

Origin
Outside the physical universe

Doctors Encountered
Ninth

Description
Ethereal, wraith-like creatures

10
9
8
7
6
5
4
3
2
1

Fear Factor
8/10

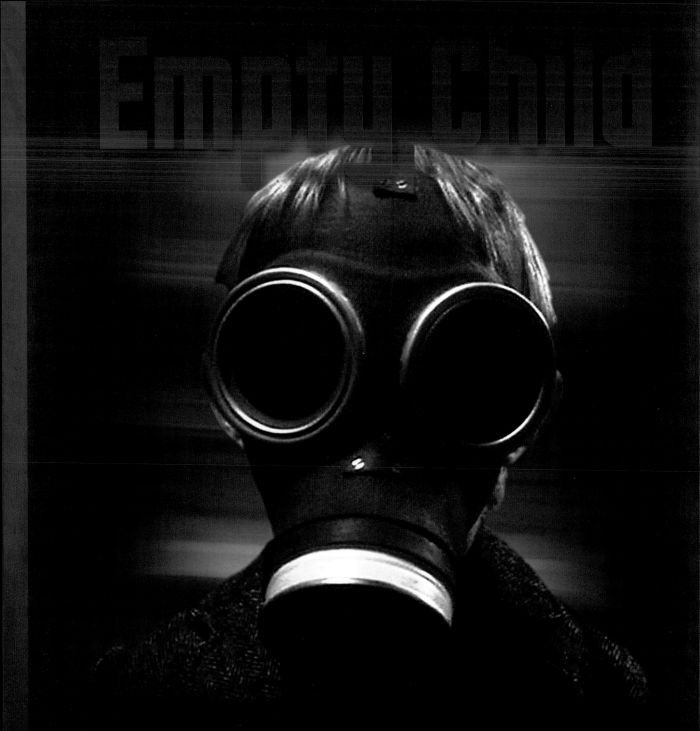

Empty Child

During the London blitz, alien nanogenes from a Chula hospital vessel found the dead body of a small boy and tried to repair him. The nanogenes are tiny, microscopic devices programmed to repair Chula Warriors on the battlefield. Believing the dead boy to be 'normal' the nanogenes used his body as a template for 'repairing' any humans they come into contact with – fusing gas masks to the victims' faces, and recreating the exact same injuries...

Origin
Planet Earth

Doctors Encountered
Ninth

Description
A small boy wearing a gas mask

Just as the child, Jamie, was desperate to find his mother, so the other infected people also became, in effect, small children searching for their mummy. The Ninth Doctor was able to provide a genuine and accurate human 'template' for the nanogenes, in the form of Jamie's mother, so they could then repair him properly along with the other infected humans.

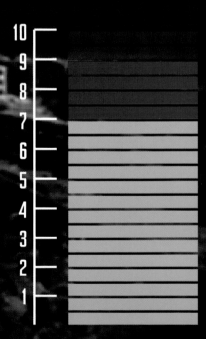

10
9
8
7
6
5
4
3
2
1

Fear Factor
9/10

Savage creatures from outside time itself, the Reapers take advantage of points in time and space where time itself has been damaged in some way. They are drawn to these 'wounds', like bacteria. But unlike bacteria they sterilise the wound, which they do by destroying everything inside it – not good if you happen to be near a space/time problem.

The Reapers

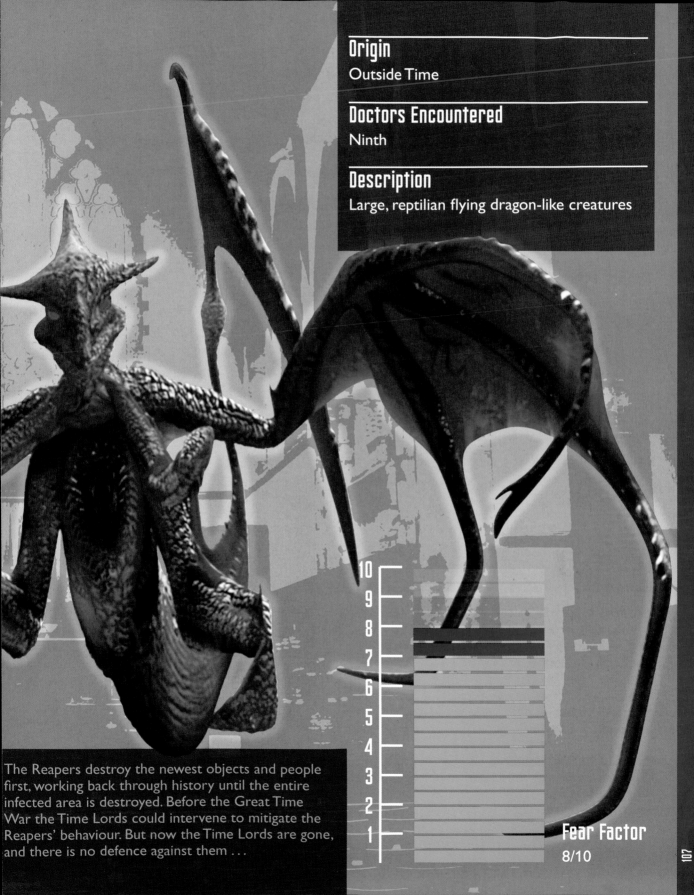

Origin
Outside Time

Doctors Encountered
Ninth

Description
Large, reptilian flying dragon-like creatures

The Reapers destroy the newest objects and people first, working back through history until the entire infected area is destroyed. Before the Great Time War the Time Lords could intervene to mitigate the Reapers' behaviour. But now the Time Lords are gone, and there is no defence against them ...

Fear Factor
8/10

Slitheen

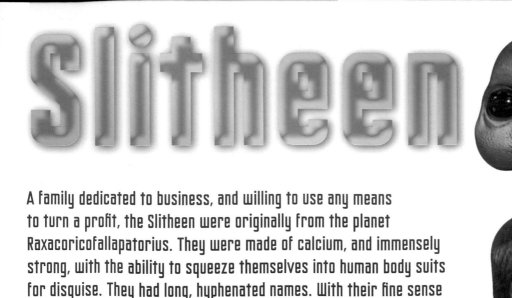

A family dedicated to business, and willing to use any means to turn a profit, the Slitheen were originally from the planet Raxacoricofallapatorius. They were made of calcium, and immensely strong, with the ability to squeeze themselves into human body suits for disguise. They had long, hyphenated names. With their fine sense of smell, they hunted ritually, enjoying the chase.

Seeing the potential Earth offered as a commodity, once purged of its population and reduced to a radioactive energy source, the Sltheen determined to stage a hostile takeover. They took the place of members of the UK authorities hoping to spark a nuclear war that would leave the planet as a source of fuel they could sell.

The Doctor and his friend Sarah Jane Smith have encountered the Slitheen, and other Raxacoricofallapatorians, like the Blathereen, on several occasions.

Origin
Planet Raxacoricofallapatorius

Doctors Encountered
Ninth

Description
Large, pot-bellied, green calcium-based life form

10
9
8
7
6
5
4
3
2
1

Fear Factor
8/10

The Doctor has described the Nestene Consciousness as 'a ruthlessly aggressive intelligent alien life form.' The Nestenes have no actual form of their own, and adapt to suit the current environment. The Consciousness is made from living plastic – able to take on any form.

Nestene Consciousness

The Nestenes have tried to colonise Earth several times. The first time, the Third Doctor thwarted their plan to take over using Autons disguised as shop-window dummies. With the help of UNIT, he defeated the Master's attempt to bring in a Nestene invasion force.

Origin
Nestene Home World

Doctors Encountered
Third, Ninth

Description
Living plastic

The Ninth Doctor first met Rose Tyler while tracking down the Nestene Consciousness. Its food stock planets had been destroyed in the Great Time War, and again it fixed on Earth as a target for conquest. But the Doctor managed to destroy it using anti-plastic.

10
9
8
7
6
5
4
3
2
1

Fear Factor
6/10

Autons

Crude weapons with a single offensive function, the Autons were the troops of the Nestene Consciousness. The Autons looked like life-sized plastic dummies, and were often disguised as shop-window mannequins. The Nestenes could channel their awareness and intelligence into suitable vessels, and plastic was an ideal host. A small portion of Nestene Consciousness animated each Auton.

More advanced Autons could be made to resemble – and imitate – real people, like Mickey Smith or Rory Williams. Each Auton had a gun concealed inside its hand – the fingers dropping away to allow it to fire. Bullets and even shotguns had no effect on the Autons.

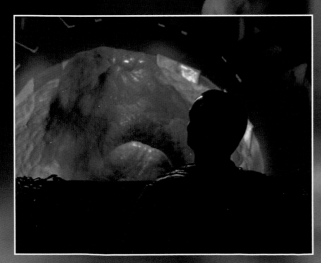

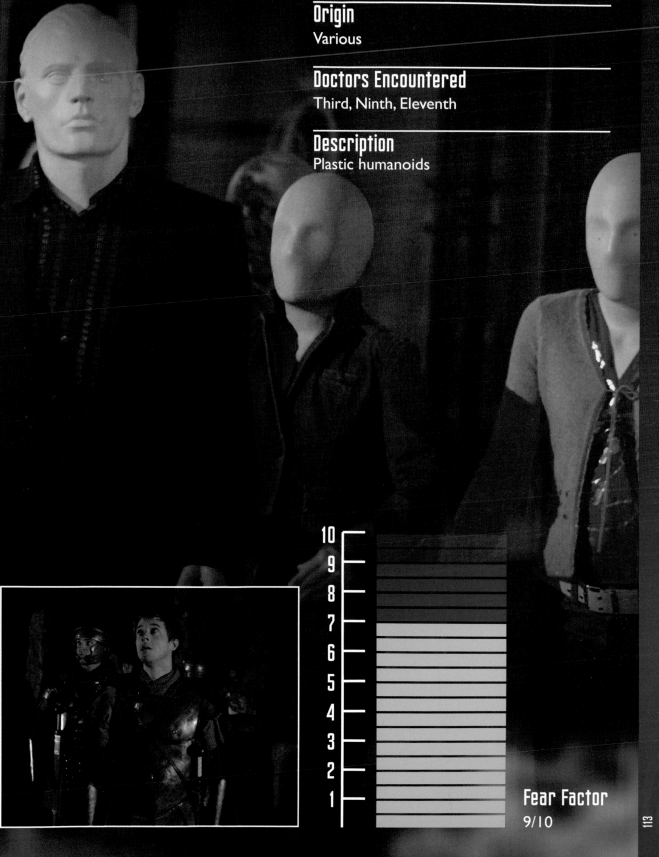

Origin
Various

Doctors Encountered
Third, Ninth, Eleventh

Description
Plastic humanoids

10
9
8
7
6
5
4
3
2
1

Fear Factor
9/10

War Machines

The War Machines were armoured mobile computers built by the super-computer WOTAN – which stood for Will Operating Thought Analogue. WOTAN was housed in the Post Office Tower (now the BT Tower) high above London, and decided it could run Earth more efficiently than humans.

WOTAN was to be the hub computer of a global network – like the Internet, only many years earlier in the 1960s. It was able to hypnotise people and make them do what it wanted – it could even take control of them through the telephone. Having taken over its creator, Professor Brett, WOTAN then ordered the War Machines to be built, to take over the world's capitals.

The First Doctor was able to defeat WOTAN only by reprogramming a War Machine to return to the Post Office Tower and destroy the supercomputer.

Origin
Planet Earth

Doctors Encountered
First

Description
Armoured robotic vehicles

Fear Factor
5/10

Zarbi

The Zarbi were a giant cross between ants and beetles that lived on the now-barren planet Vortis. They were not intelligent, and lived at peace with the other inhabitants of Vortis, like the Menoptra – intelligent butterfly-like creatures.

Origin
Planet Vortis

Doctors Encountered
First

Description
Large ant-beetle insects

The Zarbi were made militant by the dark power of the Animus, a parasitic creature that came to Vortis and infected the whole planet. Its fungal structure spread across Vortis and the Menoptra were forced to flee the planet. But with the help of the Doctor and his friends, the Menoptra were able to return to Vortis and destroy the Animus. With the controlling force gone, the Zarbi once more became docile.

10
9
8
7
6
5
4
3
2
1

Fear Factor
5/10

YETI

When a formless entity known as the Great Intelligence tried to manifest itself in the mountains of Tibet in the 1930s, it created robot abominable snowmen – Yeti – to carry out its plans. The Intelligence was defeated by the Doctor with the help of the monks of Det-Sen Monastery and an English explorer called Professor Travers.

Origin
Planet Earth

Doctors Encountered
Second

Description
Huge, robotic furry beasts

With the Intelligence defeated, Travers brought a deactivated Yeti and other artefacts back to London and forty years later, the Intelligence was strong enough to try again. This time it sent its robot Yeti into the London Underground where it had set a trap for the Doctor. But again the Doctor was able to defeat the Intelligence, this time with the help of the British army, led by Colonel Lethbridge-Stewart who would become a firm friend and head of UNIT in the UK.

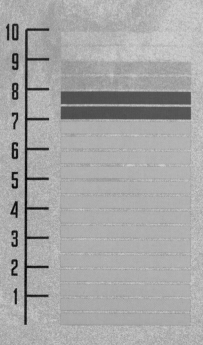

Fear Factor

8/10

Krotons

The Krotons were a crystalline life form that could survive for long periods in the form of a dormant slurry. This slurry could be reactivated by mental energy, returning to intelligent form.

A Kroton Dynatrope crashed on the planet of the Gonds, and not enough of the crew survived to repair and pilot the ship – which was powered by mental energy. The Krotons returned to crystalline slurry, leaving learning machines that would educate the Gonds to the point where their mental powers would be useful. The most brilliant Gond students were taken into the Dynatrope and drained of their mental energy – eventually reanimating the two surviving Krotons.

The Second Doctor was able to destroy the Krotons by adding acid to their crystalline slurry, in effect poisoning them. The Gonds used more acid to destroy the Dynatrope.

Origin
Unknown

Doctors Encountered
Second

Description
Tellurium-based crystalline life form

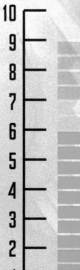

Fear Factor
6/10

Family of Blood

A short-lived species, the so-called Family of Blood came to Earth in 1913, hunting for the Doctor. Their plan was to absorb the Doctor's Time Lord essence so that they could live forever. They hunted by a strong sense of smell, and kept in contact with each other telepathically.

Origin
Unknown

Doctors Encountered
Tenth

Description
Unknown, but they assume other forms

Having traced the Doctor to Earth, they stole bodies from local people so they were disguised while they hunted for him – as they had no idea what he looked like. They also used molecular fringe animation to create an army of deadly scarecrows that they used to attack the school where the Doctor was hiding, having made himself temporarily human.

Fear Factor
8/10

Scarecrows

Hunting for the Doctor, the Family of Blood tracked him to Earth. Here they brought an army of Scarecrows to eerie life by use of molecular fringe animation. They used the Scarecrows as their troops in the battle to find and capture the Doctor.

The Scarecrows abducted humans so that the Family could steal their bodies to use as disguises. The Scarecrows were also used to attack Farringham School for Boys when the Family of Blood traced the Doctor there – though the Doctor had taken on a disguise of his own as History teacher, John Smith.

The Scarecrows ceased to have any life of their own when the Family was defeated by the Doctor.

Origin
Planet Earth

Doctors Encountered
Tenth

Description
Scarecrows brought to life by fringe animation

Fear Factor

8/10

Quarks

The Quarks were the deadly robot servants of the cruel Dominators, so-called Masters of the Ten Galaxies. The Dominators' war mission was to spread and colonise other planets – taking prisoners back to their home planet as slave labour, so as to make more Quarks available for the war effort.

Short, brutal robots, the Quarks had weaponry built into their folding arms and powerful sensor equipment. They were powered by ultrasound, which they also used as a weapon. The Quarks spoke in a high-pitched voice and communicated with each other using high-pitched beeps and squeals.

The Second Doctor encountered the Quarks when the Dominators tried to enslave a peace-loving race on the planet Dulkis, and turn their planet into a huge fuel store for their battle fleet.

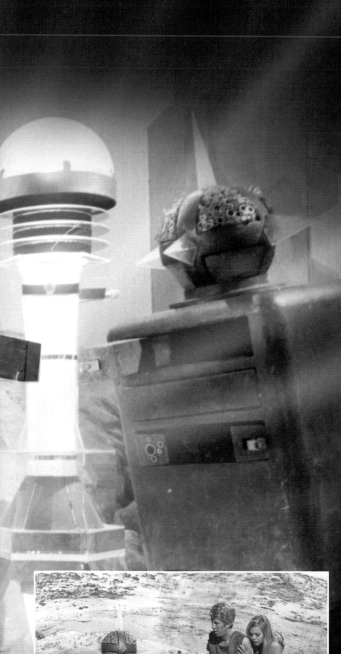

Origin
The Ten Galaxies

Doctors Encountered
Second

Description
Armoured box-like robots with spiked heads

10
9
8
7
6
5
4
3
2
1

Fear Factor
7/10

GIANT SPIDERS

When an Earth spacecraft crashed on the planet Metebelis Three, the survivors were unable to repair their ship or signal for help, and settled on the planet. But an ordinary spider from the ship found its way into the mountains of blue crystal that could enhance the power of the mind . . . The spiders became cleverer and larger, and eventually took control of the settlers.

Origin
Metebelis Three

Doctors Encountered
Third

Description
Giant spiders

Ruled by Queen Huath, the spiders sought the last great crystal of power for 'The Great One' – an enormous spider who wanted the crystal to complete a lattice that would amplify her own brain waves and make her the most powerful creature in existence . . . But the final crystal had been taken years earlier by the Third Doctor, who defeated the Great One at the cost of one of his own lives.

Fear Factor
7/10

DRACONIANS

Ruled by an hereditary Emperor, the Draconians were a race steeped in honour and tradition. They did not lie, and females were not permitted to speak in the presence of their 'betters', such as the Emperor.

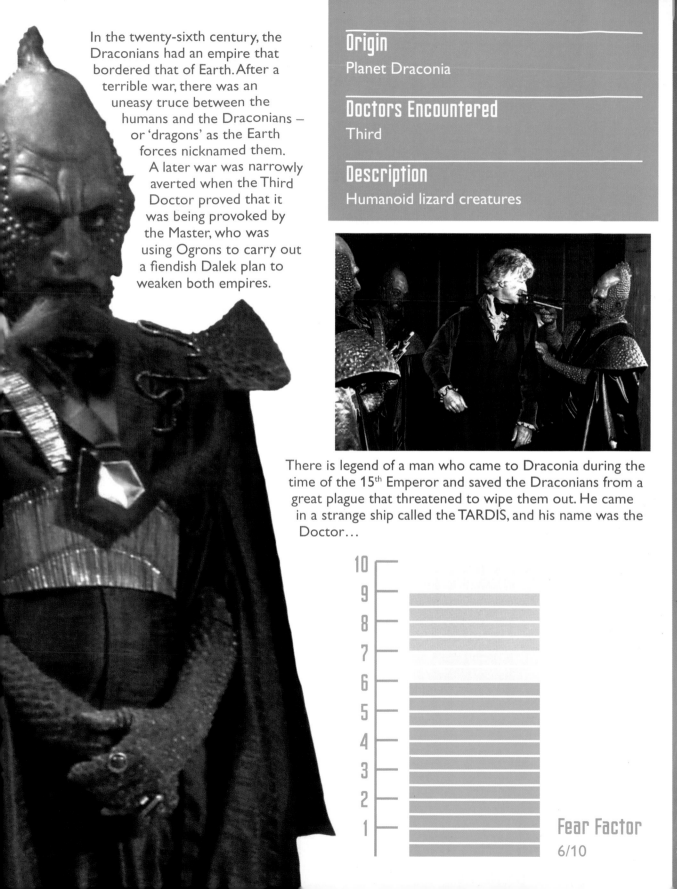

In the twenty-sixth century, the Draconians had an empire that bordered that of Earth. After a terrible war, there was an uneasy truce between the humans and the Draconians – or 'dragons' as the Earth forces nicknamed them.

A later war was narrowly averted when the Third Doctor proved that it was being provoked by the Master, who was using Ogrons to carry out a fiendish Dalek plan to weaken both empires.

Origin
Planet Draconia

Doctors Encountered
Third

Description
Humanoid lizard creatures

There is legend of a man who came to Draconia during the time of the 15th Emperor and saved the Draconians from a great plague that threatened to wipe them out. He came in a strange ship called the TARDIS, and his name was the Doctor...

10
9
8
7
6
5
4
3
2
1

Fear Factor
6/10

AXONS

Axos was a huge space parasite that landed on planets and hastened their destruction by absorbing the energy from the planet. Axos fed on this energy, using it to survive.

When the Master guided Axos to Earth, the parasite pretended to be a giant organic spaceship with a crew of Axons. These Axons were the humanoid (or semi-humanoid) manifestations of the composite creature Axos. At first they appeared to be beautiful, benevolent gold-skinned humanoids. But in their true form as parts of Axos itself, they were revealed as blobby, tentacled creatures that were immune to bullets and could kill at a touch. The Axons could absorb energy and transmit it back to Axos — one Axon was able to transfer the entire output of a nuclear reactor.

The Doctor was only able to defeat Axos with the help of his old enemy the Master.

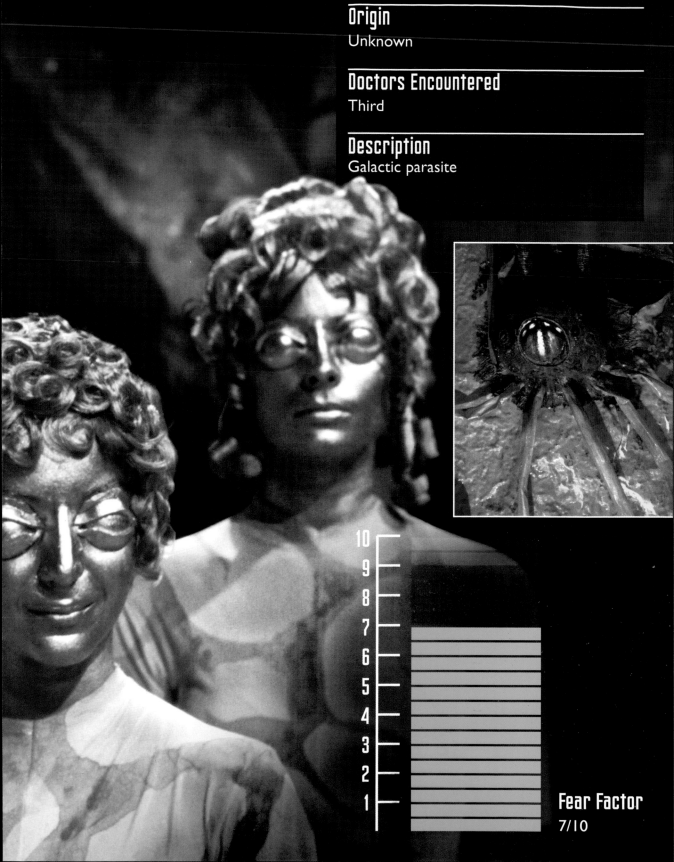

Origin
Unknown

Doctors Encountered
Third

Description
Galactic parasite

10
9
8
7
6
5
4
3
2
1

Fear Factor
7/10

Adherents of the Repeated Meme

The Ninth Doctor and Rose encountered the Adherents of the Repeated Meme when they witnessed the final end of the world on Platform One. The Adherents were apparently from Financial Family Seven, reciting their 'Meme' at thirty-minute intervals, in whispering graveyard voices.

Little or nothing of their features could be seen under their hooded cloaks, except for their part-metal, part-organic claws. But as the Doctor discovered, the Adherents were not all that they seemed, and were in fact created by Lady Cassandra as a way of smuggling her robotic spider servants onto the Platform as 'gifts'.

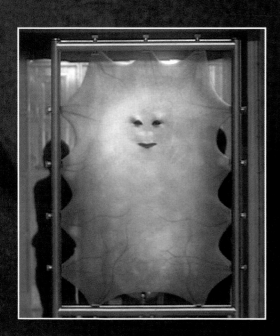

Origin
Fictitious

Doctors Encountered
Ninth

Description
Cloaked and hooded humanoids

10
9
8
7
6
5
4
3
2
1

Fear Factor
5/10

Cassandra

The Lady Cassandra O'Brien Dot Delta Seventeen claimed to be the last pure-bred, Earth-born human. As a result of all the 'beauty' treatments and plastic and genetic surgery she underwent, she eventually became a flat piece of skin stretched over a metal frame, her brain floating in a tank of life-support fluid below.

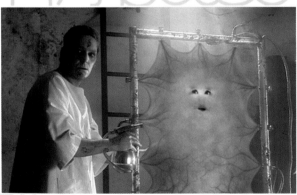

A shrewd businesswoman, Cassandra tried to sabotage Platform One, hoping to make a profit from the resulting crisis. But the Ninth Doctor and Rose thwarted her plan and it seemed she was killed.

The Tenth Doctor and Rose later encountered Cassandra again on New Earth – where she attempted to steal first Rose's body and then the Doctor's. Finally, the Doctor and Rose were able to help Cassandra find peace and contentment before she died.

Origin
Planet Earth

Doctors Encountered
Ninth, Tenth

Description
Skin stretched over a metal frame

Fear Factor

6/10

New Earth Patients

The Sisters of Plenitude on New Earth were responsible for the health care of the citizens. But to find cures for previously incurable diseases and ailments, the Sisters created specially grown humans who they infected with every known disease, so as to make them living incubators for new cures. Because they were the carriers of the diseases, they did not die from them.

The patients were kept perpetually conscious in individual sealed booths, fed with pipes bearing nutrients and oxygen, and yet more disease.

Cassandra released the patients, who in fact only wanted to be loved. But in the hospital's sterile atmosphere, their touch was fatal. Luckily, the Tenth Doctor was able to devise a cure for the multiple diseases, while staying away from the patients long enough to administer it.

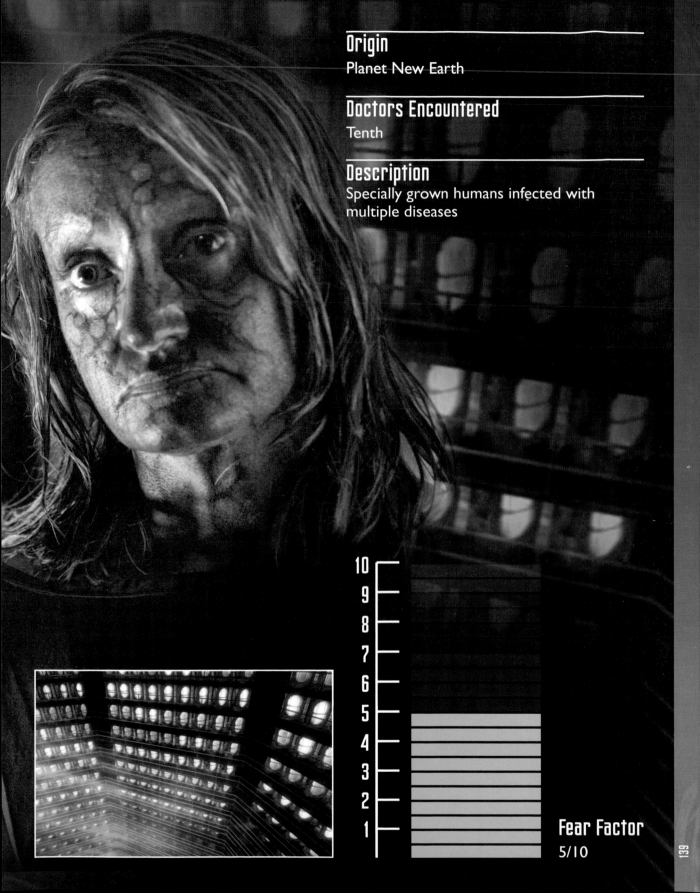

Origin
Planet New Earth

Doctors Encountered
Tenth

Description
Specially grown humans infected with multiple diseases

10
9
8
7
6
5
4
3
2
1

Fear Factor
5/10

Cat People of New Earth

By the year five billion, with the original Earth abandoned and then destroyed when the sun expanded, humans adopted a planet in the galaxy M87 as 'New Earth'.

Origin

New Earth

Doctors Encountered

Tenth

Description

Humanoid felines

The planet's most advanced medical facility was the hospital outside the city of New New York run by the cat-like Sisters of Plenitude. The Sisters took a life-long vow to help others and to minister to and heal the sick. Humanity is a challenge for them, as it is afflicted with so many diseases. Within the hospital, the Sisters could – miraculously – cure even the most virulent and previously untreatable diseases and conditions. But the Doctor discovered their cures came at a terrible cost ...

Returning to New New York years later, the Doctor met other Cat People, trapped in a huge traffic jam along with humans, and prey to the terrible Macra.

10
9
8
7
6
5
4
3
2
1

Fear Factor

5/10

Macra

Once an intelligent race that enslaved others in order to get the gas they needed to survive, by the time the Tenth Doctor encountered them on New Earth the Macra had been reduced to instinctive, unthinking animals.

The Second Doctor met the Macra at an earlier stage in their development – when they enslaved a human colony. The Macra brainwashed the colonists into believing the gas they needed was valuable and essential to the colony. The colonists then mined the gas for the Macra, who secretly controlled and regulated the humans' lives.

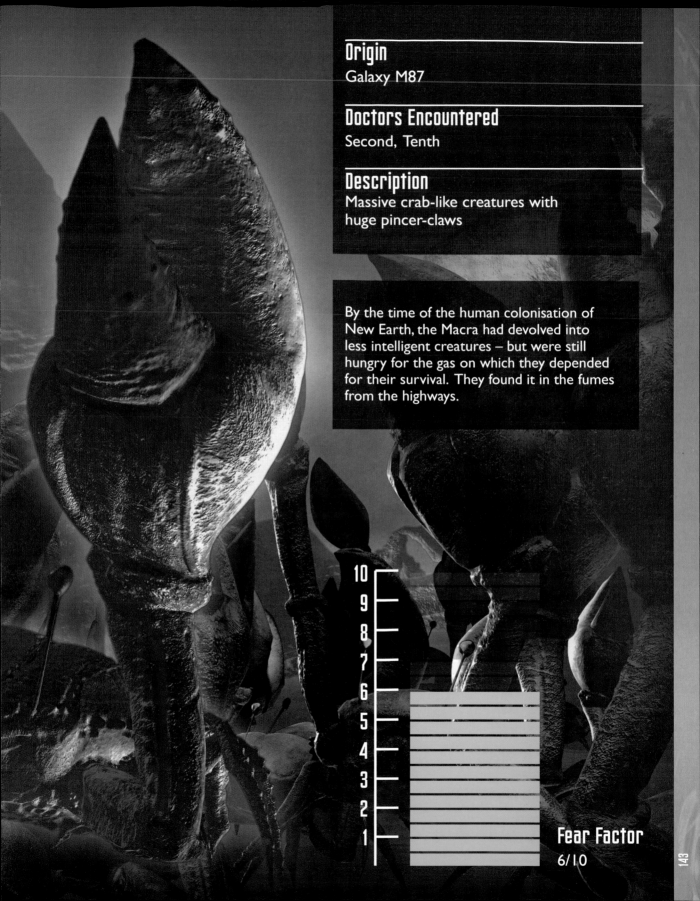

Origin
Galaxy M87

Doctors Encountered
Second, Tenth

Description
Massive crab-like creatures with
huge pincer-claws

By the time of the human colonisation of
New Earth, the Macra had devolved into
less intelligent creatures – but were still
hungry for the gas on which they depended
for their survival. They found it in the fumes
from the highways.

10
9
8
7
6
5
4
3
2
1

Fear Factor
6/10

Aggedor

Once the royal beasts of Peladon lived on the slopes of the holy mountain, Mount Mageshra. Their fur was used to trim the royal robes and their features formed the emblem of royalty. But the creatures were hunted almost to extinction.

When the Third Doctor visited Peladon, there was only one of the creatures remaining alive – Aggedor. High Priest Hepesh used the creature to attack his enemies in an attempt to keep Peladon from joining the Galactic Federation. He claimed the deaths were caused by the angry spirit of the royal beast, but the Doctor pacified the creature and revealed the truth.

Fifty years later, the Doctor and Aggedor met again when the Ice Warriors tried to take control of the planet. Aggedor helped track down a dangerous criminal, but was killed saving Queen Thalira who was held hostage.

Origin
Planet Peladon

Doctors Encountered
Third

Description
Savage royal beast of Peladon

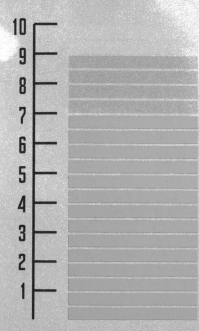

Fear Factor
7/10

Dæmons

The Dæmons originated on the planet Damos – 60,000 light years from Earth – and first came to Earth nearly 100,000 years ago. Glimpsed throughout history, they secretly helped man to evolve and have entered myth as the traditional image of the devil – perhaps building on the race-memories of the Beast.

The Dæmons' psionic science has been part-remembered as magic and superstition. But to the Dæmons, human evolution and development was simply an experiment. If humanity failed that experiment, then the Dæmon left on Earth would destroy the world. That Dæmon was Azal, who was reawakened by the Master, who hoped to inherit the Dæmon's power. But instead, Azal decided to pass on his awesome power to the Doctor – who refused it.

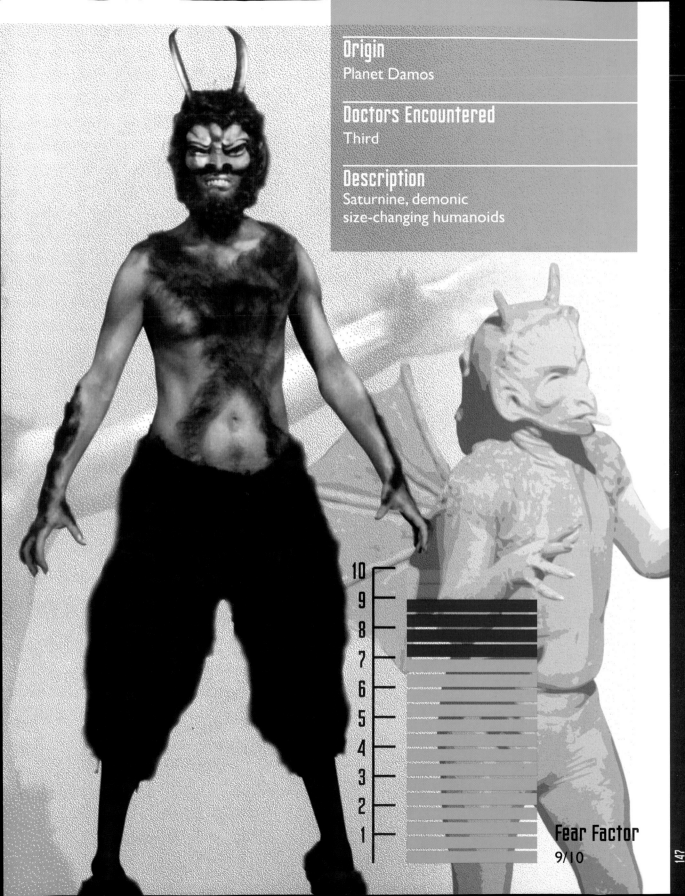

Origin
Planet Damos

Doctors Encountered
Third

Description
Saturnine, demonic
size-changing humanoids

10
9
8
7
6
5
4
3
2
1

Fear Factor
9/10

Wirrn

The large, insect-like Wirrn lived in deep space, returning to a planet to breed and lay eggs inside cattle. When the Wirrn larvae emerged, they fed on the 'host' in which the eggs were laid.

After humans destroyed the Wirrn's breeding colonies, a lone Wirrn Queen found Space Station Nerva and laid her eggs inside one of the humans held in cryogenic suspension there. The Wirrn that were born absorbed not just food, but also the knowledge of their 'host'. They also infected other people, absorbing their knowledge and turning them into Wirrn. It was only with the help of the Fourth Doctor that the waking humans were able to fight off the Wirrn.

Origin
Andromeda

Doctors Encountered
Fourth

Description
Upright insectoid, with deadly sting

10
9
8
7
6
5
4
3
2
1

Fear Factor
8/10

Robots of Death

The Fourth Doctor and Leela encountered a
robot-dependent society when they arrived on
a huge sandminer searching for valuable ores
and minerals in a vast desert. The small human
crew was served by three types of robot –
non-speaking, single-function robots called
Dums, more sophisticated Voc class robots
and a controlling Super Voc – SV7.

Each robot was identified by type and number –
for example V17 or D84 – and programmed
to obey the human crew. Each Voc-class robot
had more than a million multi-level constrainers
which prevented it from being able to harm
humans. But, as the Doctor and Leela
discovered, the roboticist Taren Kapel had
learned how to override these constraints,
and the robots rebelled.

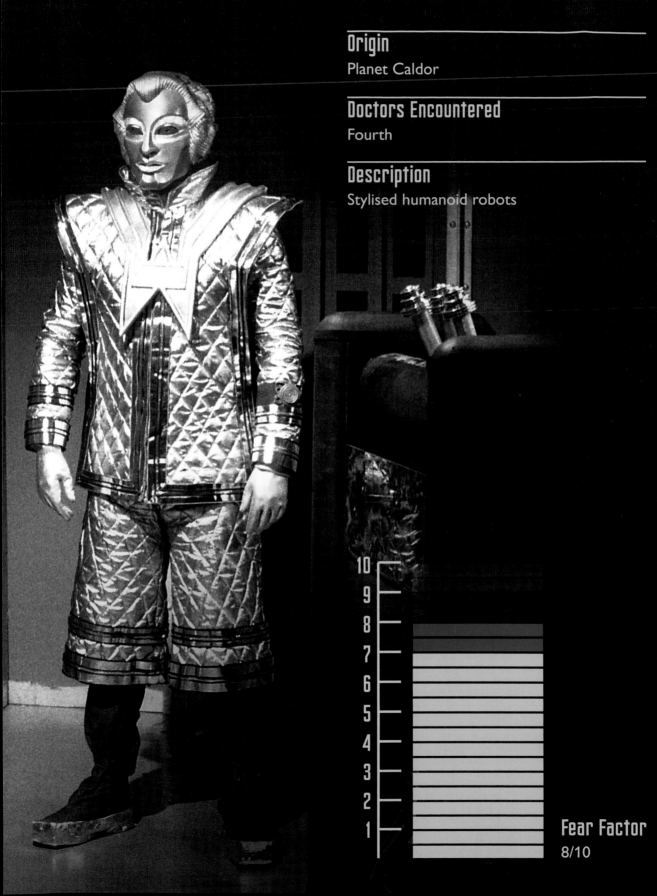

Origin
Planet Caldor

Doctors Encountered
Fourth

Description
Stylised humanoid robots

Fear Factor

8/10

10
9
8
7
6
5
4
3
2
1

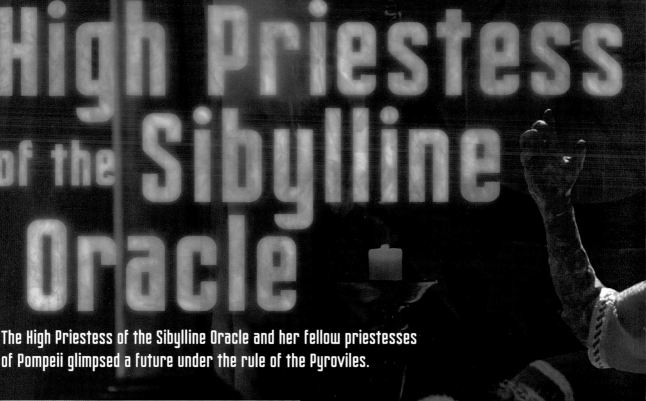

High Priestess of the Sibylline Oracle

The High Priestess of the Sibylline Oracle and her fellow priestesses of Pompeii glimpsed a future under the rule of the Pyroviles.

That future took a step towards becoming reality as the High Priestess breathed in contaminated vapours from Mount Vesuvius. The vapours mutated the priestesses, slowly turning them to stone, like the Pyroviles. The High Priestess, perhaps breathing more of the vapours, mutated further and faster. By the time the Doctor met her, she had gone a long way towards becoming a Pyrovile – a hideous creature made of stone. As she was made of fire, the Doctor was able to fend her off with a water pistol!

Origin
Ancient Pompeii

Doctors Encountered
Tenth

Description
Human priestess turned to fiery stone

10
9
8
7
6
5
4
3
2
1

Fear Factor
6/10

Pyroviles

Humans in the nearby Roman town of Pompeii breathed in Pyrovillian dust dispersed through the hypocausts from Mount Vesuvius. This was slowly turning them to stone – making them become Pyroviles. These included the Sisters of the Sibylline Oracle, whose High Priestess was turned completely to stone.

The Pyroviles were a race made of rock and fire and all their technology derived from these same elements. Escaping from the destruction of Pyrovillia, a group of Pyroviles made their way to Earth almost two thousand years ago, making their base deep inside Mount Vesuvius in Italy.

The Pyroviles planned to weld themselves to humans – creating a new species, and boiling away Earth's oceans and seas. The Tenth Doctor and Donna were able to stop the Pyroviles, but could not save the people of Pompeii from the eruption of Mount Vesuvius.

Origin
Planet Pyrovillia

Doctors Encountered
Tenth

Description
Creatures of rock and fire

10
9
8
7
6
5
4
3
2
1

Fear Factor
7/10

Kraals

When their planet Oseidon became too radioactive, the Kraals decided to conquer another planet and make it their own – Earth. The Kraals planned to replace key figures in a Space Defence Station and the nearby village of Devesham with androids. Having bypassed Earth's defences, the androids would then release a virus that would kill everyone, before becoming inactive when Marshal Chedaki's invasion fleet arrived.

To train the androids, the chief Kraal scientist Styggron created a duplicate defence station and village. When the Fourth Doctor and Sarah Jane Smith arrived, they thought at first they were in the real Devesham. Despite encountering android copies of themselves, the Doctor and Sarah Jane were able to get to Earth to warn UNIT of the danger. The Doctor reprogrammed his own android to kill the Styggron and prevent the release of the deadly virus.

Origin
Planet Oseidon

Doctors Encountered
Fourth

Description
Grey-skinned rhinocerids

10
9
8
7
6
5
4
3
2
1

Fear Factor
6/10

Zygons

The Zygons were an alien race from a planet destroyed by a stellar explosion. A vast refugee fleet was assembled when the catastrophe struck, but had nowhere to go. A group of Zygons had already crash-landed in Scotland centuries ago and remained hidden while awaiting rescue. Led by Warlord Broton, these Zygons decided to make Earth into a new Zygon homeworld.

Origin
Distant planet destroyed by solar flares

Doctors Encountered
Fourth

Description
Orange-brown and covered with nodules

Their greatest weapon was the Skarasen – a huge cyborg creature that had lived with them in Loch Ness. The Zygons used the Skarasen to destroy North Sea oil rigs as a test of strength, before planning to hold the world to ransom. But the Doctor and UNIT were able to destroy the Zygons and their ship. With no new orders, the Skarasen returned to Loch Ness.

Fear Factor
7/10

Fendahl

Millions of years ago on an unnamed planet, evolution went up a blind alley and a creature evolved that fed on life itself – even its own life. The Fendahl was a creature that consumed life – it was death itself. Having destroyed all life on the lost Fifth Planet of Earth's solar system, the Fendahl was thought to have been destroyed when the planet blew up. The Time Lords put a time loop round the planet to keep the Fendahl captive, but it had already escaped and found its way to Earth.

The Fendahl was a gestalt-creature – a composite of twelve Fendaleen and a Core. Each component was created from living matter or mental energy. On Earth, the Fendahl lay dormant within a skull until energy from time experiments released it. While dormant, it influenced evolution so that humans became a suitable creature for the Fendahl to absorb to create itself.

Origin
Unknown

Doctors Encountered
Fourth

Description
A composite, gestalt creature that *is* death

Fear Factor

8/10

Mr Sin

A ventriloquist's dummy used by magician Li H'Sen Change in his Victorian music-hall act, Mr Sin was in fact the Peking Homunculus – a robot creature brought back from the fifty-first century by escaping war criminal Magnus Greel.

The Peking Homunculus was made as a toy for the children of the Commissioner of the Icelandic Alliance in the year 5,000. It contained a series of magnetic fields operating on a printed circuit and a small computer as well as one organic component – the cerebral cortex of a pig. But the pig's brain took over the Homunculus, and the swinish instinct became dominant – it hated humanity and revelled in carnage.

Origin

Planet Earth

Doctors Encountered

Fourth

Description

Murderous ventriloquist's dummy

Back in Victorian London, Mr Sin's instinctive nature drove it to rebel against its master Greel. Greel was killed, and the Fourth Doctor deactivated Mr Sin.

10
9
8
7
6
5
4
3
2
1

Fear Factor

9/10

The Resurrected Master

Once the Doctor and the Master were friends – they were even at school together. But after he looked into the Untempered Schism, the Master became a psychopathic megalomaniac.

During the Great Time War, the Master fled and hid, disguising his true identity even from himself. But with his memory restored, he used the Toclafane to conquer Earth. When the Tenth Doctor and Martha defeated him, the Master was killed and the Doctor cremated his body on a great funeral pyre.

But the Master was restored to life by a group of fanatical followers. It was only a half-life, and he kept reverting to a tortured, skeletal form. Finally, the Master discovered that as a child he had been deliberately driven mad by the Time Lords who implanted a sound in his mind – a constant drumbeat – that would allow them to survive the Great Time War. In a final act of repentance and revenge, the Master sacrificed himself to ensure the Time Lords were destroyed in the war. But he has returned from the dead before …

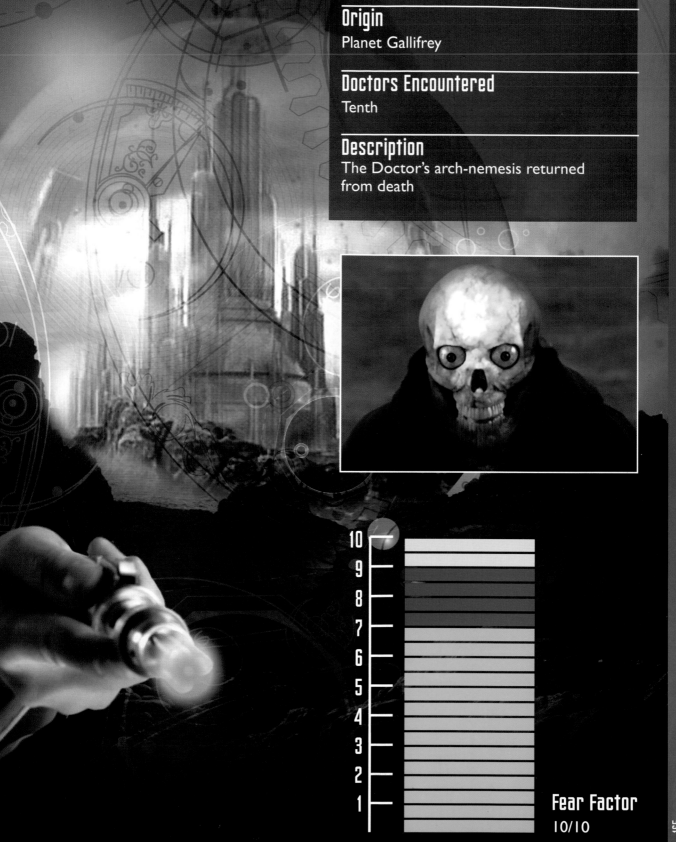

Origin
Planet Gallifrey

Doctors Encountered
Tenth

Description
The Doctor's arch-nemesis returned from death

Fear Factor
10/10

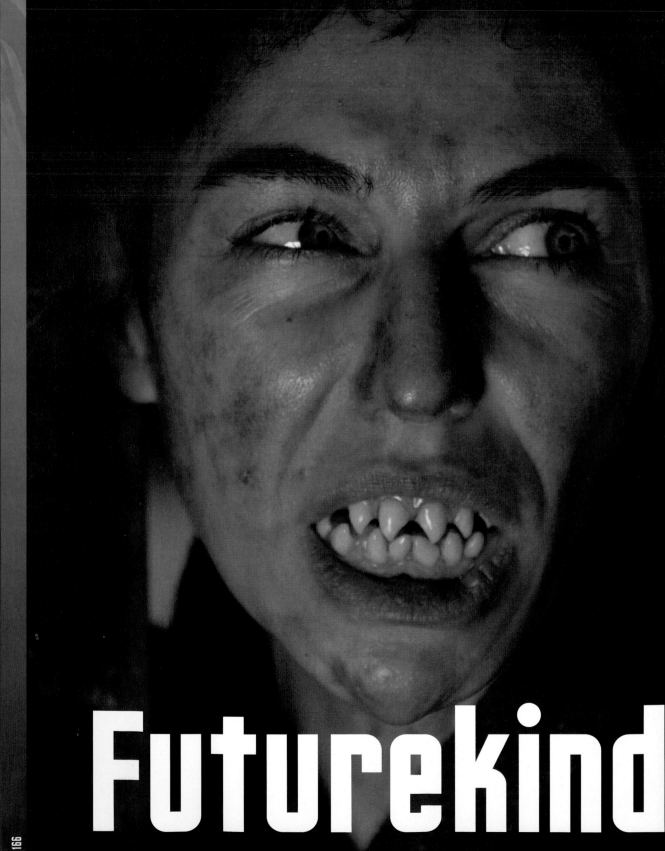

Futurekind

Futurekind were the mutated savages that the human race might become if it degenerates. They had fanged teeth, painted their bodies and hunted anything they could eat. They even hunted other, non-mutated humans.

Origin
Planet Malcassairo

Doctors Encountered
Tenth

Description
Mutated future humans

The Doctor, Martha Jones and Captain Jack Harkness encountered Futurekind on the planet Malcassairo in the distant future. Other survivors of the human race had taken shelter inside a huge silo, where they had built their rocketship. They hoped this would take them to Utopia where they could find other survivors of humanity. But in fact, this was where the last survivors became the Toclafane.

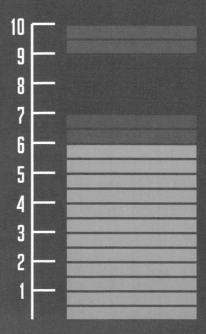

10
9
8
7
6
5
4
3
2
1

Fear Factor
6/10

Toclafane

The Master called the aliens he brought to Earth 'the Toclafane' but the Tenth Doctor knew this was a name he had made up from Time Lord mythology.

The Toclafane were technologically advanced spheres, about the size of a football, that spoke in sing-song voices rather like naughty children. They hovered and flew through the air and could emit deadly pulses of energy, as well as using knives and cutting tools that slid out from their round casings.

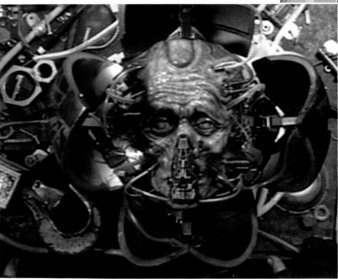

While the Toclafane appear to be mechanical, inside each is a withered, disembodied human head plugged into the mechanisms. This is what the human race will become in order to survive on Utopia billions of years in the future. They were brought back to the present by the Master to conquer the Earth and rule over their own ancient ancestors.

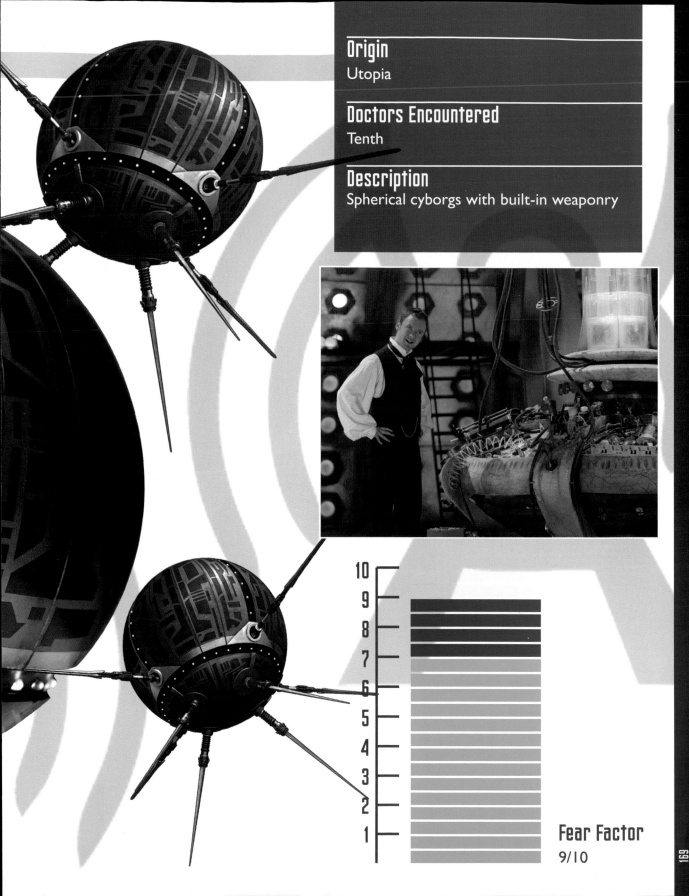

Origin
Utopia

Doctors Encountered
Tenth

Description
Spherical cyborgs with built-in weaponry

Fear Factor
9/10

Krynoid

A carnivorous plant species, the Krynoids could infect and absorb animal life – using people as plant food. The Krynoid plant grew inside an animal – or human – 'host' turning them into a plant. They also had the ability to channel their powers of mobility and aggression to other plants. On planets where the Krynoid settled, all animal life soon became extinct.

The Fourth Doctor encountered two Krynoids that came to Earth as pods, then grew. The first was destroyed at an Antarctic scientific base. But the second pod was grown into a full Krynoid by millionaire plant lover Harrison Chase. The Doctor was able to call in UNIT to help destroy the Krynoid.

Origin
Unknown

Doctors Encountered
Fourth

Description
Deadly plant life

Fear Factor
8/10

Giant Robot

Built to replace humans in difficult and dangerous operations such as deep mining or exploring alien planets, experimental robot K-1 was reprogrammed by its creator Professor Kettlewell to help the Scientific Reform Society in its attempt to take over control of Earth.

But the Robot reacted against the programming, and accidentally killed Kettlewell – which drove the Robot insane. Although the newly-regenerated Fourth Doctor and UNIT had prevented the SRS plan to launch nuclear weapons and start a war, the Robot determined to go through with it. The Brigadier tried to destroy the Robot with a disintegrator gun, but being made of a new 'living' metal, the Robot absorbed the energy and grew to giant size. The Doctor eventually destroyed the Robot with a virus that attacked the 'living' metal.

Origin
Created by Professor Kettlewell

Doctors Encountered
Fourth

Description
Functional prototype robot made of 'living' metal

10
9
8
7
6
5
4
3
2
1

Fear Factor

6/10

Mummies

The walking mummies that the Fourth Doctor and Sarah Jane Smith encountered were actually Osiran Service Robots. They were wrapped in bandages impregnated with chemicals to stop the robots from corrosion, and were controlled by the imprisoned Osiran criminal Sutekh.

Sutekh was the last survivor of the Osirans — a devious and cunning race. A force for evil, he destroyed his own planet and was finally caught on Earth by the surviving Osirans led by Horus. Defeated, Sutekh was imprisoned beneath a pyramid, unable to move. The power source for his prison was the Eye of Horus, housed in another pyramid on Mars.

But when Egyptologist Marcus Scarman found Sutekh's 'tomb', Sutekh was able to use his immense mental powers to control Scarman and have him use Osiran service robots to build a missile that would destroy the Pyramid of Mars and free Sutekh from his ancient bonds.

Origin
Planet Phaester Osiris

Doctors Encountered
Fourth

Description
Bandage-wrapped service robots

Fear Factor
8/10

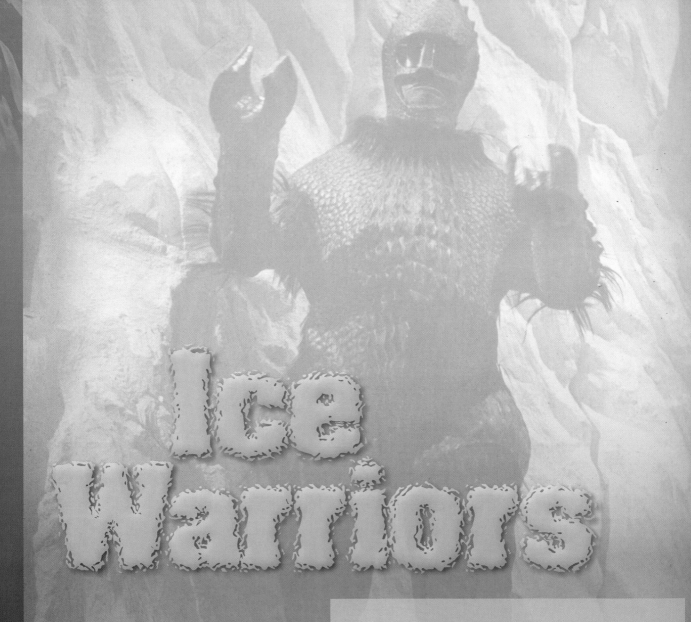

Ice Warriors

Original inhabitants of the planet Mars, these tall reptilian bipeds were nicknamed Ice Warriors because of their aversion to heat. After Mars became uninhabitable, they tried to make Earth their home – planning to adjust the climate and kill the human population. But in the far future, the Ice Warriors will become allies of humanity, joining the Galactic Federation.

The Ice Warriors have a long tradition of nobility and honour. It is this appetite for 'death or glory' that led a group of Ice Warriors fronted by Lord Azaxyr to turn on the Federation and side with their enemies in Galaxy Five. But their plot was discovered and defeated by the Doctor.

Origin
Planet Mars

Doctors Encountered
Second, Third

Description
Reptilian humanoid in armoured shell

10
9
8
7
6
5
4
3
2
1

Fear Factor
8/10

Ice Lord

The Martian nobility, sometimes termed Ice Lords, were less armoured than the Ice Warriors they commanded, and had a more streamlined helmet. Steeped in honour, the Ice Lords were formidable and cunning commanders.

The Second Doctor defeated Lord Slaar's attempt to invade Earth and use Martian seed pods to adapt its climate so that Ice Warriors could live there but humans would die. The Third Doctor worked with Lord Izlyr to unmask a traitor within the Galactic Federation on the planet Peladon. Later he encountered the cruel Lord Azaxyr – leader of a breakaway group of Ice Warriors who wanted to abandon the path of peace and return to the days of death or glory . . .

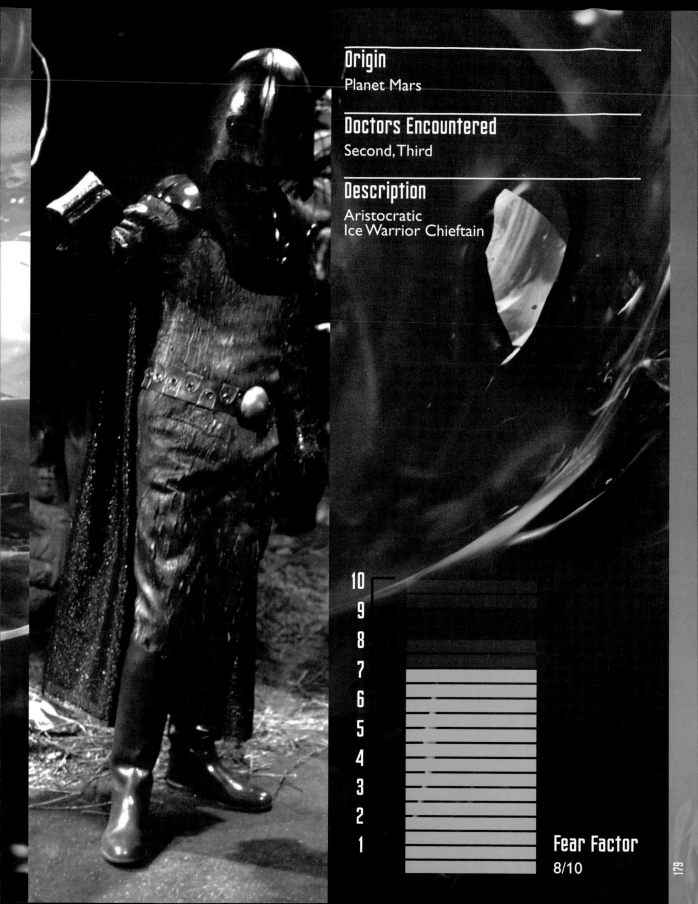

Origin
Planet Mars

Doctors Encountered
Second, Third

Description
Aristocratic
Ice Warrior Chieftain

10
9
8
7
6
5
4
3
2
1

Fear Factor
8/10

OGRI

Several Ogri were illegally brought to Earth by the criminal Cessair of Diplos when she escaped from her prison ship. She hid them in an existing ancient stone circle called The Nine Travellers, although there were more than nine stones.

Origin
Planet Ogros

Doctors Encountered
Fourth

Description
Silicon-based life forms that look like rocks

he Ogri needed amino acids and protein to
urvive – which can be found in blood plasma.
hey could move, and were able to absorb the
ood from anyone who touched them. They
ere also 'fed' animal blood by the worshippers
f the ancient Celtic goddess the Calleach –
ho was actually Cessair. The Fourth Doctor
rranged for the Ogri to be returned home
 the Megara, justice machines that were
esponsible for transporting Cessair of Diplos
r trial.

Fear Factor
8/10

Terileptils

The Terileptils were a reptilian race and renowned for their love of art and beauty. Most were peaceful, but convicted Terileptil criminals were sent to work in the tinclavic mines on Raaga. Many of them sustained injuries and scarring as a result.

A small group of Terileptils managed to escape and sought refuge on Earth. Although they could survive in Earth's own atmosphere for a considerable time, they used a soliton gas generator to provide an atmosphere more suitable for Terileptil lungs.

They also used both mind control and an android dressed as the figure of Death to keep the local population under control. The Terileptils planned to release an enhanced variant of bubonic plague (the Black Death) to kill off the human population of Earth. But the Fifth Doctor and his friends were able to defeat them and their plague was destroyed by the great fire of London in 1666.

Origin
Vicinity of Raaga

Doctors Encountered
Fifth

Description
Upright reptiles

10
9
8
7
6
5
4
3
2
1

Fear Factor
7/10

Sil

Sil was a particularly sycophantic and
repugnant Mentor from the planet Thoros Beta.
He was sent to the planet Varos to negotiate the
yearly price-review for Galatron Mining prior
to a new contract. Galatron Mining had been
buying from Varos – and exploiting them – for
centuries. With a taste for marsh minnows, and
needing to be moisturised constantly in Varos's
atmosphere, Sil's eccentric speech patterns
were due to a fault in his language transposer.

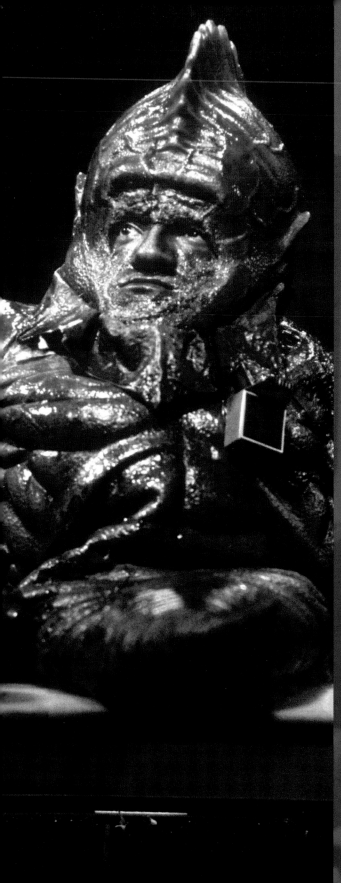

Origin

Thoros Beta

Doctors Encountered

Sixth

Description

Large, slimy, slug-like creature

Enjoying the trials and tortures that took place in the Punishment Dome on Varos, Sil took an instant dislike to the Doctor. The feeling was mutual, and the Doctor was eventually able to help the Governor of Varos break free of the Mentor's control. The Doctor later encountered Sil on his home planet.

10
9
8
7
6
5
4
3
2
1

Fear Factor

6/10

Haemovores

If Fenric, a being of pure evil, has his way, then thousands of years in the future the human race will evolve into Haemovores – mutated creatures with an insatiable appetite for blood.
The Haemovores will be born out of the pollution of the post-industrial age, but Fenric has manipulated time so that people have been infected and become Haemovores since Viking times.

Origin
Planet Earth

Doctors Encountered
Seventh

Description
Mutated vampiric humans

Once infected, the victims become pale vampire-like figures. But over time they mutate into hideous, grey-green creatures that can live in the sea. Their destiny is bound to the will of Fenric – they are his 'wolves' – and predicted by the legends of Norse mythology. The 'infection' has followed the journey of the flask in which Fenric is imprisoned and which was stolen by Viking raiders . . .

10
9
8
7
6
5
4
3
2
1

Fear Factor
7/10

Ogrons

Strong but with limited intelligence, the ape-like Ogrons lived on one of the Outer Planets. They worshipped and feared a large, shapeless monster that also lived on the planet. Because of their strength and mindless obedience, the Ogrons were often used by other races as mercenaries. The Daleks in particular have used Ogrons as part of the occupying force for planets they have conquered.

Origin
Outer Planets of the Galaxy

Doctors Encountered
Third

Description
Ape-like humanoids

The Daleks used Ogrons as security troops to keep the human population of Earth under control after their invasion in the twenty-second century. They also allowed the Master to use the Ogrons to try to provoke a war between Earth and the Draconian Empire in the twenty-sixth century.

10
9
8
7
6
5
4
3
2
1

Fear Factor
7/10

Jagrafess

The real authority in charge of
Satellite Five and all its broadcasting and
communications during the Fourth Great
and Bountiful Human Empire was the Mighty
Jagrafess. The Editor of Satellite Five answered
to the Jagrafess – a huge creature stretched
out across the ceiling and roof of the control
room on Floor 500 of Satellite Five. From the
moment that Satellite Five went online,
ninety-one years before the Doctor arrived,
the Jagrafess guided and shaped mankind
using the satellite's news reports.

By manipulating the news,
the Jagrafess was able to
create a climate of fear –
even to create an enemy
who did not exist. It could
use subliminal messaging
to subvert the economy or
change a vote. It was playing
a long game, manipulating
events for its own profit
and for the benefit of its
secret allies. It was not until
the Doctor returned to
Satellite Five many years after
destroying the Jagrafess that
he realised it was working
for the Daleks.

Origin
The Holy Hadrojassic Maxarodenfoe

Doctors Encountered
Ninth

Description
Huge shapeless creature with teeth

10
9
8
7
6
5
4
3
2
1

Fear Factor
8/10

Pig Slaves

The Cult of Skaro, while trapped in New York in 1930, experimented with the genetic structure of the human race. One result of this was the Pig Slaves. The Daleks took ordinary human beings – like the unfortunate Laszlo, a stage hand at the Lorenzo Theatre – and turned them into creatures that were half human, half pig.

Origin
Planet Earth

Doctors Encountered
Tenth

Description

Humans and pigs adapted to be slaves by the Daleks

The Daleks also brainwashed these creatures, so that they became unquestioning servants of the Daleks, ready to steal more humans for them. The less intelligent humans were turned into pig slaves, while the cleverer ones were destined to take part in the 'Final Experiment' and become Human Daleks.

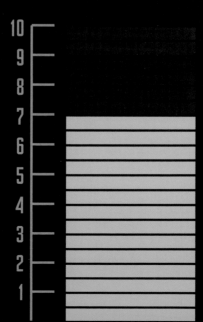

10
9
8
7
6
5
4
3
2
1

Fear Factor
7/10

DALEKS

The Daleks are the most hated, feared and dangerous life form in the Universe. Mutated and genetically engineered survivors of a terrible thousand year war, the Dalek Creature exists inside a travel machine casing that provides life-support and armament.

EX-TER-MI-NATE
EX-TER-MI-NATE
EX-TER-MI-NATE
EX-TER-MI-NATE

Origin
Planet Skaro

Doctors Encountered
First, Second, Third, Fourth, Fifth, Sixth, Seventh, Ninth, Tenth, Eleventh

Description
Mutant creature inside armoured casing

The Daleks are not only perfectly adapted for waging war, they are cunning and ruthless scientists, too. They have developed time travel technology that rivals the Time Lords – to the point where both races waged the terrible Great Time War that seemed to destroy them. But the Daleks, it seems, are never utterly defeated and have returned once again to fulfil their destiny of universal conquest and domination.

10
9
8
7
6
5
4
3
2
1

Fear Factor
10/10

Emperor Dalek

The supreme leader of the Daleks is their Emperor. The Emperor Dalek has taken several forms throughout Dalek history.

The Second Doctor was taken to Skaro on the orders of a huge Dalek Emperor built into the very heart of the Dalek City. It was destroyed when the Doctor provoked a Dalek civil war. The Emperor Dalek encountered by the Seventh Doctor turned out actually to be Davros, housed inside a specially adapted Imperial Dalek casing.

After the Great Time War the Dalek race was apparently wiped out. But the Ninth Doctor found there were survivors, commanded by an Emperor that – having led its people from the wilderness and created new Dalek life – believed itself to be the god of all Daleks. This enormous Dalek Emperor was wired into the Daleks' flagship, and destroyed by Rose Tyler when she unleashed the raw force of the Time Vortex.

Origin
Planet Skaro

Doctors Encountered
Second, Seventh, Ninth

Description
The supreme ruler of the Dalek race

Fear Factor
10/10

Human Dalek Sec Mutant

The Daleks of the Cult of Skaro escaped from the Battle of Canary Wharf using an emergency temporal shift. They ended up in New York in 1930, where they tried, and failed, to create new Dalek embryos. Forced to adopt another plan, the Daleks genetically adapted human beings to become Dalek-like.

The leader of the Cult of Skaro, Dalek Sec, was genetically bonded with Mr Diagoras, the man in charge of completing the Empire State Building. The Daleks had seen his ambition and drive, and his determination to control New York made him an ideal candidate for the experiment. Using a chromatin solution to facilitate the process, Diagoras was pushed into the flesh of the Dalek Sec creature, and the two became one.

To survive, the Cult of Skaro reasoned, the Dalek species must evolve and experience life outside their shells – the children of Skaro must walk again.

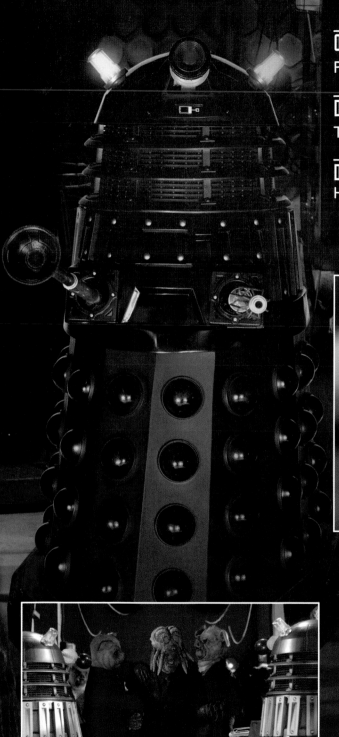

Origin
Planet Skaro

Doctors Encountered
Tenth

Description
Humanoid/Dalek hybrid with single eye

10	
9	
8	
7	
6	
5	
4	
3	
2	
1	

Fear Factor
9/10

Mad Dalek Caan

The last survivor of the fabled Cult of Skaro, Dalek Caan tried to return to the Great Time War that had all but destroyed the Dalek race. The Time War was time-locked, but after countless attempts, Dalek Caan escaped.

Dalek Caan arrived just as Davros's command ship flew into the jaws of the Nightmare child at the Gates of Elysium. The effort of breaking the time-lock, and the things that Dalek Caan witnessed in the Vortex drove Caan mad. But he achieved his mission – he saved Davros.

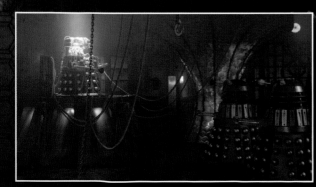

Origin
Planet Skaro

Doctors Encountered
Tenth

Description
Insane Dalek creature inside a shattered Dalek casing

Dalek Caan used the knowledge and insight he gained from within the Time Vortex itself to predict the future. He foresaw the arrival of the Doctor – the Threefold Man, the Dark Lord – and his precious Children of Time on the Dalek Crucible. He knew that one of these Children of Time would die, just as he knew the Daleks themselves were doomed ...

10
9
8
7
6
5
4
3
2
1

Fear Factor
8/10

Davros

Towards the end of the terrible thousand year war between the Kaleds and the Thals on the planet Skaro, a Kaled scientist called Davros found a way for his race to survive the war and the mutating effects of the chemical, biological and radioactive weapons that had been used.

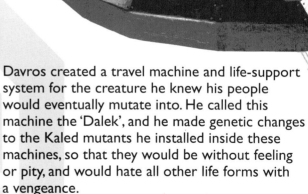

Davros created a travel machine and life-support system for the creature he knew his people would eventually mutate into. He called this machine the 'Dalek', and he made genetic changes to the Kaled mutants he installed inside these machines, so that they would be without feeling or pity, and would hate all other life forms with a vengeance.

The Daleks he had created rebelled against Davros, and exterminated him. But Davros was not killed, and has returned again and again to help his creations in their aim to conquer all life in the Universe.

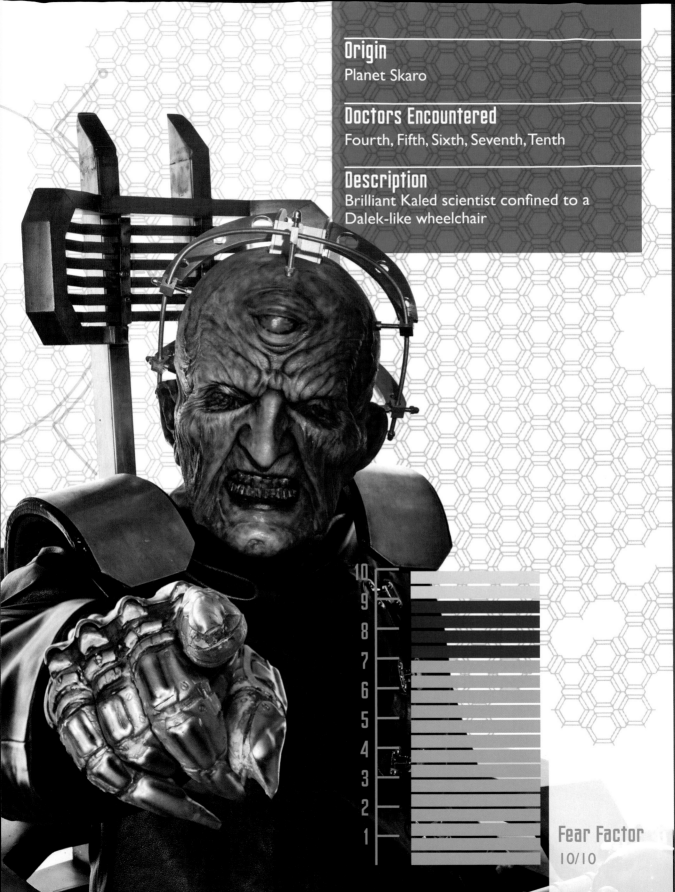

Origin
Planet Skaro

Doctors Encountered
Fourth, Fifth, Sixth, Seventh, Tenth

Description
Brilliant Kaled scientist confined to a Dalek-like wheelchair

10
9
8
7
6
5
4
3
2
1

Fear Factor
10/10

Ironsides

Apparently developed by scientist Edwin Bracewell, the 'Ironside' was a motorised war machine supposedly designed to defeat the Nazis. But despite being repainted, its lights blacked out, and a munitions belt strapped round it, Winston Churchill instinctively recognised an alien threat. The Ironsides were actually Daleks that wanted Churchill to send for the Doctor – because they needed him to recognise them for what they really are.

The Daleks were able to use the Doctor's recognition as proof that they really were Daleks, and activate a Progenitor device that created a new race of Daleks – a new Dalek Paradigm. Despite the Doctor's and Churchill's efforts – including an attack by Spitfires adapted for space flight, the Daleks escaped to create a new race of Daleks . . .

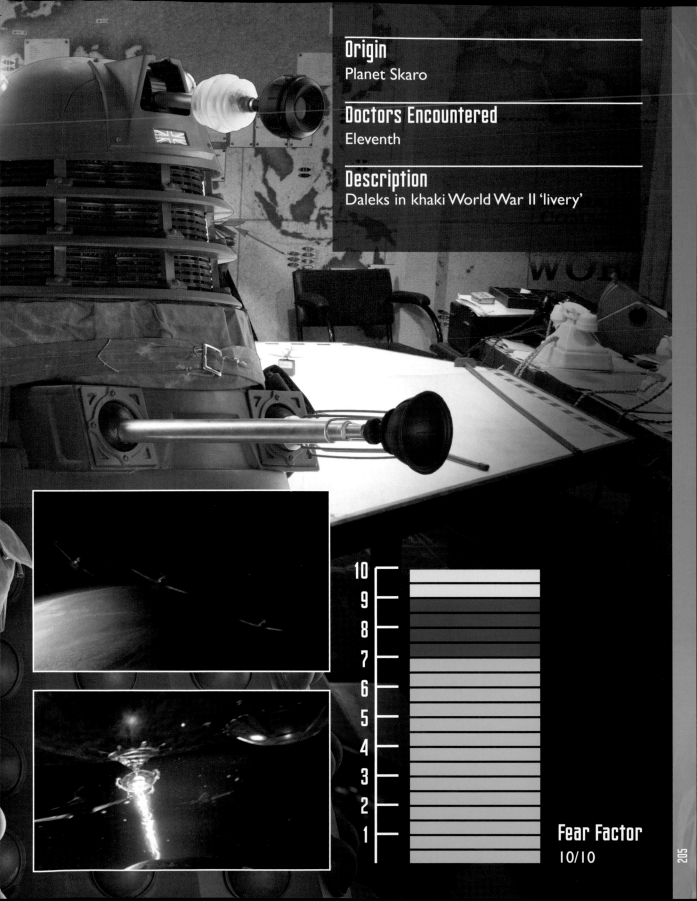

Origin
Planet Skaro

Doctors Encountered
Eleventh

Description
Daleks in khaki World War II 'livery'

Fear Factor
10/10

10
9
8
7
6
5
4
3
2
1

NEW DALEK PARADIGM

Before the Great Time War between the Daleks and the Time Lords, the Daleks seeded the universe with Progenitor Devices – each holding a genetic copy of the 'pure' Dalek race.

A group of Daleks that survived the Great Time War recovered one of these Progenitor Devices, but could not activate it as the device did not recognise them as pure Dalek. So they tricked the Doctor into confirming that they were indeed Daleks. With the Doctor's confirmation, the Daleks' Progenitor device created a new Dalek Paradigm – from the original Dalek genetic code.

Origin

Planet Skaro

Doctors Encountered

Eleventh

Description

Enlarged armoured pepper-pot shape

These new 'officer-class' Daleks have redesigned, larger casings. As well as a new Dalek Supreme, the progenitor also creates archetypal Daleks of each rank – including the blue Strategist Dalek, orange Scientist Dalek, yellow Eternal Dalek and red drone Dalek.

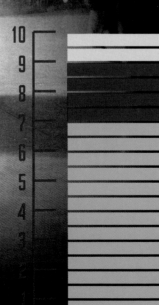

Fear Factor
10/10